D0940255

Duck Thief
& Other Stories

Duck Thief
& Other Stories

DAVID P. LANGLINAIS

4519 0622
East Baton Rouge Parish Library
Baton Rouge, Louisiana

2015
University of Louisiana at Lafayette Press

© 2015 by University of Louisiana at Lafayette Press
All rights reserved

ISBN 13 (paper): 978-1-935754-64-0

http://ulpress.org
University of Louisiana at Lafayette Press
P.O. Box 40831
Lafayette, LA 70504-0831

Printed on acid-free paper in South Korea.

Book cover design: Bryan Pudder
Cover photography: Jeanine Michna-Bales
Portrait photo: Teresa Hall at Wild Wind Photography

Library of Congress Cataloging-in-Publication Data

Langlinais, David.
[Short stories. Selections]
Duck thief & other stories / David Langlinais.
pages cm
Summary: "A collection of short stories set in South Louisiana"
Provided by publisher.
ISBN 978-1-935754-64-0 (alk. paper)
1. Louisiana--Fiction. I. Title. II. Title: Duck thief and other
stories.
PS3612.A5845A6 2015
813'.6--dc23
2015016618

For My Juliette

Contents

{1}

Duck Thief

Two weeks ago the juvenile mallards began disappearing. First at Mr. Piazza's. Then Mr. Dubois lost some and so did Mr. LaCroix and Mr. Broussard. That's when Ted LaPierre's father came up with the idea of building the duck pen on the bank of the bayou behind the house. Using scrap-wood, Ted and his father constructed a four-foot-square frame then wrapped chicken wire around it. That evening, when they were feeding the flock, Ted and his father herded together as many ducks as they could, about thirty, corralling them into the makeshift structure.

And now here Ted sits with a shotgun in the dark in the middle of the night, hiding in the shadows of the oak tree that blocks the light of the full moon. Everything has a strange green glow to it. He isn't wearing insect repellent because he doesn't want to alert the duck thief to his presence. Mosquitoes buzz at his ears. He hasn't moved in two hours.

The ducks in the pen are no longer aware of him the way they appeared to be earlier. Still, they're unsettled. Ted watches them, their heads raised, turning in jerks toward sounds or movement he can't distinguish. He knows they don't like being exposed in the night.

"So, what exactly am I waiting for again?" Ted had asked as he came out at midnight to relieve his father. It was Ted's last night at home, and he didn't want to spend it squatting behind a tree in the backyard with a shotgun in his hands. He would be flying out the next day.

"You'll know when you see him," his father said, moving as if stiff and in pain, scratching at mosquito bites the size of coins that had risen on his hands and neck. He'd been crouching under the tree since eight that evening.

"And what am I supposed to do if it comes to that?" Ted asked.

"You'll know that, too."

———

Mr. Piazza had recently bought thirty new mallards. The ducks weren't quite old enough to be out on their own yet, so for the time being he had them in the small pen in his backyard. Not long before that, Mr. Dubois had bought two dozen mallard eggs and was hatching them in an incubator he had borrowed from Mr. Bertrand who, a few weeks earlier, had added to the flock an exotic breed of duck he called Indian Runners—strange, long-necked birds that were shaped like bowling pins and really didn't look anything like a duck. The geese were for Mr. LaCroix, a whole flock of them. There were ducks and geese everywhere up and down the bayou on Eleazar Street.

Earlier that year, Ted's father had contributed three dozen mallards and ten of the large white domestic Pekin ducks to the flock. He'd nailed a wooden duck house to each of the four willow trees in the backyard so that they hung well out over and above the bayou, just as wood ducks preferred it, just as the Wildlife and Fisheries recommended. When the eggs hatched and the ducklings were old enough, they would leave the houses, dropping the ten feet to the water below, as if it were better escaping the threat of chicken snakes and opossums for the many dangers awaiting them in the water.

An hour has passed and Ted wishes he'd worn longer and thicker socks. It would have been a good idea to wear hip boots. But he hadn't thought it through. Now he sits on the grass and the roots, bugs all around him, mosquitoes eating him alive. Ted could tell his father was too excited to sleep and knows he might be watching from the living room window. Otherwise, Ted would move to one of the lawn chairs on the patio. Ted knows his father wouldn't be happy if he found him sitting anywhere but under the tree and in the hiding spot they'd both agreed on. He already didn't think Ted was taking the situation seriously. So Ted puts the chair out of his mind and continues to stay low, blending in with the shadows.

During the night, most of the ducks slept under a restaurant about a half-mile up river. The restaurant was a large wooden structure built on stilts against the floods that came once or twice a year in the spring and sometimes again in the fall during hurricane season. In the hours after midnight the ducks, all 150 or so, left the safety of the restaurant and moved in thick rafts up the bayou and back to the yards where they played and chased one another. The big drakes ganged up on and tried to screw the young hens. The ducks made a commotion until dawn came and the neighborhood men fed them corn.

Ted found it hard to sleep in his old bedroom, which looked out on the bayou. The ducks made loud, raspy quacking calls, magnified in the still air over the water. After he did fall asleep, he was often awakened by the arrival of the geese that came at first light and moved down the bayou in a crowded flotilla, heads held high and announcing themselves with a chorus of honks.

"God, it's beautiful, isn't it?" his father had said on Ted's first morning home. They were in the kitchen and his father was laughing, thinking it funny that Ted had been kept awake. His parents' bedroom faced Eleazar Street—they never heard the ducks.

"Beautiful? How the hell does anyone sleep around here?" Ted had always been cross in the morning. Even after a good night's sleep.

"Oh, you get used to it," his father said, still laughing, leaning on the kitchen counter where the newspaper was spread open. He took a tentative sip from a mug that had steam rising from it. Ted grabbed a cup from the cabinet and poured himself some coffee.

"What are they doing out there anyway?" Ted said, still mad about the ducks.

"They're playing," his father said, like it was an obvious thing. "It's what ducks do."

"Why can't they play behind someone else's—"

He was interrupted by the sound of a lawn mower cranking up outside. Ted's father stopped laughing and glanced at his watch.

"Dammit, what are they doing here so early?" he said. Then he quickly drained what was left in his mug, like it was cold lemonade and not hot coffee. He set the mug next to the sink and moved toward the back door. "They're gonna scare off my ducks before I even have a chance to feed 'em."

Ted followed his father outside with his coffee, moving toward the carport in his bare feet. It didn't feel like fall, but then it didn't feel like summer anymore either—it was neither cool nor hot—and he watched his father approach the man on the riding mower. It was Mr. Fontenot. He mowed the LaPierre's yard. Until a year ago, he had mowed most of the yards on Eleazar Street. But that was before the Sonnier twins, from just up the street, entered high school and began saving up for college. Much of the neighborhood had fallen into line, and now the Sonnier boys were mowing all but a few of the yards.

Mr. Fontenot's teenage son, Will, was taking a weed eater from the bed of the pickup. Lean and wiry like his father, Will had on the dark green coveralls they always wore on the job. Years ago, Ted's father had given Will permission to fish in the bayou behind the house anytime he wanted. In fact, Ted had fished with him on many occasions. He'd grown fond of the boy and saw a lot of potential in him.

Mr. Fontenot turned the mower off and looked at Ted's father.

"I was about to feed the ducks," Ted's father said. "You mind doing the front yard first?"

"Hey, Will?" Ted said. "Been doing much fishing?" Will smiled, showing a mouthful of large, white teeth, all crowded together and straight. He was about to answer, but the mower started up again. Then Will followed Mr. Fontenot toward the front of the house and Ted followed his father down toward the bank of the bayou, where the ducks were waiting.

———

Ted's leg has gone numb. His lower back aches. He wishes he'd brought out a cushion to sit on. The tree's roots are hard—gnarled and knobby. But he doesn't move, he wants to stay out of sight. It's why he hasn't lighted the cigar in his mouth. The cigar butt is soggy and falling apart between his teeth, and he replaces it with a fresh cigar from the top shirt pocket of his camouflaged hunting shirt.

The smoke would repel the mosquitoes. It's why he smoked in the blind before dawn whenever he went duck hunting. But he never smoked once it was shooting time. Ted is a serious hunter and, despite the discomfort, he would never do anything that might give himself away.

———

His father and the other men no longer hunted. Now they raised ducks and geese, had learned to find them too beautiful to shoot. One morning, the week before, Ted heard his father saying he wanted to kill a boy he'd seen water-skiing through ducks on the bayou behind the house.

"I was right there on the patio. But he went ahead and did it anyway," he said. "The little bastard. I shouted at him that if he ever did it again I'd shoot him. And, goddammit, I meant it too!"

"Lester, he was only having fun," Ted's mother had said. She'd always been afraid of his anger.

"Fun, hell! He wants fun? I'll show him fun! Wait'll he comes back, I'll show him!"

"So what, you're just gonna sit out there with a gun?" she said, hoping he would see how crazy he sounded.

Ted envisioned his father sitting in a lawn chair, a shotgun across his lap with the safety off.

"Maybe I will, maybe I won't," he said. "We'll just have to wait and see."

Ted stayed out of it. He thought about the times when he

was a boy and had tried water skiing through the flocks of ducks on the bayou. They weren't his father's or the neighbors' ducks—it was long before the men had changed—but someone else's farther up river. As hard as he and his friends tried, they had never succeeded in hitting any. The ducks were a lot less helpless than his father was making them out to be. And while Ted had never actually run over a duck, he wondered if anyone had ever wanted to shoot him for trying.

As he watched his father, red-faced and fuming over the incident of the skier, Ted realized how resolute he was when he'd said he would never hunt again.

"I can't shoot ducks anymore," his father explained to him his first day back home while he scattered corn on the bank of the bayou.

"It'd be like shooting one of my own," he said, speaking to the birds that scrambled in a mad pile of feathers, positioning themselves at the line of corn on the lawn. Some of the younger mallards kept to the outside of the pile, holding their still-developing wings open. Then, once catching enough of the breeze, they flapped their wings, running a little, trying to fly. They didn't lift off the ground, they didn't look as if they ever would, but it wouldn't be long before they did.

At the time, Ted still didn't understand how serious his father was about the ducks, and when Ted said something about a large mallard hen within the flock—about how it would feed an entire family it was so fat—his father had glared at him.

"What's happened to you?" Ted said.

"What?"

"It used to not be this way. You've changed."

"Things change," his father said. "People change."

"Not me," Ted said. "Not like that."

"Don't be so sure," his father said, and Ted didn't like the way it made him feel. He decided to drop the subject.

"That's Susie," his father said, sounding happy again and gesturing toward the large duck. The big hen bullied its way into the pile with its greater size and weight. It was as big as a small goose. She probably had some Muscovy in her, Ted figured, and he couldn't help thinking what a good gumbo she would make. Looking up and seeing the joy in his father's face as he fed the ducks, Ted wondered if he should have felt guilty for thinking such a thing. But he couldn't help it. He loved duck gumbo. That wasn't his fault. It was his father, after all, who had taught him to love it, his mother who had taught him how to cook it.

Ted couldn't be blamed for his love of duck hunting, either. He was brought up to love that, too. It had begun when he was eight, when he got his first shotgun for Christmas, a .410 single-shot crack-barrel. Even before that, his father took him along on hunts and he would sit in the blind, decked out in camouflage and watching, learning to identify the many different kinds of ducks. Longing for the day that he, too, could actually shoot a real shotgun, a gun that kicked and thundered when he pulled the trigger.

"Hell, it'd be like shooting Rufus," his father was saying, turning the empty bucket upside down and letting the corn dust fall to the breeze.

Ted stopped thinking about eating the big mallard hen. He looked at Rufus, his father's Labrador Retriever. Lying there in the grass, tongue out and panting, watching the ducks, trained against all instinct not to pounce. He was big and black. Bigger even than his mother, Petie, who had been Ted's dog before someone took her. That was years ago and Ted would never forget the night. He'd heard the dogs making a racket in the kennel and after a while when they didn't stop barking he went outside with a flashlight to see what was going on. At the same instant he saw Petie's kennel door open, he'd heard the outboard motor crank up. By the time he ran to the bayou the boat was already thirty yards down river, taking Petie, the silhouette of a heavy, broad-shouldered man turning away just as the flashlight's beam illuminated his backside. Ted never got another dog after that and now, seeing Rufus, was glad he didn't. Rufus didn't hunt anymore and, like the men on Eleazar Street, he'd grown fat around the middle from easy living. The dog now stayed in the house rather than the kennel. He looked bored, like it was all over but for the dying and there was nothing left to do but wait.

It was a coordinated effort. The men up and down Eleazar Street discussed the situation, compared notes and talked strategy. The thefts had been going on for nearly two weeks and now the men had begun meeting each day, checking on the status of the ducks. The morning before, Ted went with his father to Mr. Bertrand's house, the last house on the dead-end street, a mile up river.

"How'd you make out last night, Lester?" Mr. Bertrand said, walking out of his house and to the truck before it had come to a complete stop on the carport. He wore white rubber shrimping-boots and held a coffee mug.

"Okay. At least nothing seemed to be missing this morning. How 'bout you?" Ted's father said with an arm resting on the truck's open window, the short end of a cigar smoldering in his fingers.

"He still hasn't come out this way," Mr. Bertrand said, sounding disappointed. Then, "Ted, what you know, podnah?"

"Not much, Mr. Roy. How you doing?"

"Oh, we got us a duck thief, Ted."

Walking from the truck and to the house, they scattered the flock of Indian Runners that had suddenly appeared on the carport, seeming curious.

"Ain't that the damnedest thing?" Ted's father said, chuckling at the ducks that had quickly regrouped and were again in a tight bunch, looking ridiculously like a rack of bowling pins.

"Just got 'em Ted," Mr. Bertrand said of the ducks. "What you think?"

"Never seen anything like it," Ted said.

On the way into the house Ted noticed a shotgun leaning against the wall just inside the door. A 20-gauge automatic. Mr. Bertrand had a large fruit orchard, and he shot blue jays for flying near the trees. His deep freeze was full of the squirrels and rabbits that had made the mistake of venturing onto his property.

Mr. Bertrand led them out the back door and now they sat on the patio drinking coffee. The sound of a lawn mower starting up came from the front yard, the noise all at once doubling as a man riding it appeared, and then he was mowing the grass around the satsuma trees. It was Mr. Fontenot.

Just then, his son Will came around the house with the weed eater and began cutting the grass around the trees. Will looked up and saw Ted on the patio. Ted waved, but Will had already returned his attention to the work.

"Good kid," Mr. Bertrand said, having to shout over the racket. "Works his ass off, I'll tell you that. Just like his father."

Ted and his father nodded in agreement.

"Times have been tough for them," Mr. Bertrand added. "You know, with the Sonnier twins and everything. I've been trying to give 'em extra work."

A moment passed and they still watched the Fontenots cut the grass. Then Mr. Bertrand rose from his chair. "C'mon," he said, "I want to show y'all something." He led them through the orchard and to the bayou. "Would you look at that bastard?"

At first Ted thought he was looking at a large, half-submerged tree trunk, but then recognized it as a big alligator, maybe eight or nine feet long.

"Caught him playing hell with my young ducks," Mr. Bertrand explained to Ted. "Can you believe it?"

Ted knew what he meant. Alligators rarely got at the mature ducks, they were too quick. But it was a different story with the younger ducks. Especially with the ducklings that kept to the water and away from land and feral cats. The water offered no protection from alligators or the large snapping turtles that came up from behind before taking the little birds under. A hen might have a dozen ducklings following it in the morning and by afternoon, all but two or three might be gone. The predation came quickly to the young and it made Ted wonder how anything ever survived the first day, let alone the first year it took to grow up.

"Thought I killed him four months ago," Mr. Bertrand said. "Then, this morning, there he was."

"Sure he's the same one, Roy?" Ted's father said.

"Yeah, I'm sure."

Ted said, "Maybe he's the reason all the ducks have gone missing."

"Nah," Mr. Bertrand said. "He's not a problem anymore. You don't see his face?" Mr. Bertrand pointed at the gator again. "Remember I said I shot him in the head? Well at least he's blind, so I won't have to go and shoot him again. I figure he won't be messing with my birds anymore."

Ted studied the gator for a moment and, sure enough, it looked blind, at least in one eye where a scabby knot now covered its right eye socket. Still, it looked healthy for a blind alligator.

———

No longer willing to put up with the discomfort of the ground, Ted moves to the patio, feeling as stiff as his father had looked two hours earlier. He sits in a lawn chair with the shotgun lying across his lap. He doesn't care anymore if his father sees him. So what if he gets mad? Ted hasn't wanted any part of this to begin with.

Ted can understand if they were waiting in ambush for a dog thief. He's sure he'd have no problem shooting a man if he were stealing Rufus. But this prowler doesn't steal dogs. He's taking ducks.

———

Ted had taken two weeks off work and come home in the fall so he could hunt. He didn't want to miss another duck season. He had anticipated the ritual of oiling up his Ithaca 12-gauge over-and-under. He couldn't wait to hold the gun again and to feel its kick.

Ted hadn't been home in over a year; he wondered when things had changed. He phoned his parents every Saturday morning and not once did his father ever mention anything about the guns. So when Ted went into the gunroom he was surprised. His gun was still there in the big oaken gun cabinet, only now it stood alone, where fifteen other guns had once been. It had taken his father a lifetime to amass that collection.

"I sold 'em off," his father said when Ted asked what had

happened to the guns.

"But you could've at least kept the .410."

"Why?"

"Dad! It was my first gun. I swear, you start raising ducks and the next thing you know everything's changed."

"There're already too goddamn many guns on the street without all mine ending up there too."

"But that's in big cities, Dad, not in small towns like this."

"Look, I'm not going to be responsible for any more murdering. I got rid of them and that's that."

Where Ted lived now, guns were falling into the wrong hands all the time. It was a problem there. When Ted had first moved there, his parents began watching the news coming out of that city more closely. His mother knew what the weather was going to be like there every day. When his parents began hearing of the record-setting murder rate they not only became frightened for Ted, but for themselves, like they, too, were living in a city nearly 1,500 miles away. They began thinking crime was bad everywhere.

But at least his father did save the Ithaca. Ted was thankful for that. It was a fine gun. His father always said he'd give it to him one day and now he had, just as promised. As Ted cleaned the gun, ram-rodding a piece of oiled cloth through the upper barrel, he wondered whom he could call. He had several friends in town that hunted. Still, there was no one Ted enjoyed hunting with more than his father and he was continuing to struggle with the notion of never going out with him again. His father had taught him everything he knew about hunting: calling ducks, building a blind, working a dog with hand signals, about leading and hitting a teal in a fast cross-flight pattern. He had never felt closer to his father than when they hunted together. When Ted thought about him, his father was often in camouflage coveralls and hip boots, smoking a cigar, sharing coffee from the thermos with him in the blind on all those rainy, bitter-cold mornings. That was always a fine time. And although he had shared many memories with his father outside of the marsh, it was those of hunting with him that he chose to recall.

———

Everyone on the bayou who lost ducks said they wanted the duck thief killed. Ted can't believe they mean it, knowing that only a year earlier, when things were different, they probably wouldn't have. But now there's someone hiding with a gun in every yard up and down the bayou, watching a pen of ducks just like Ted.

He hears something. It comes from behind him and not the bayou. At first, Ted assumes it's his father coming out of the house. But then he catches a glimpse of the figure in the periphery of his vision, moving from the direction of the carport and toward the bayou, and it startles him. Even in the dark, Ted can tell it isn't his father and he feels his grip tightening on the gun. He clicks the safety off and remains motionless. He wants to see what the prowler will do next.

Ted loses sight of him as he enters the shadows of the oak tree. Then he emerges, moving animal-like along the bayou before turning toward the duck pen. Ted stands up and, in the same motion, brings the gun up to his shoulder. He levels his aim on the duck thief.

"Okay, hold it right there," Ted says in a soft, sure voice.

The prowler freezes and looks up. He says, "Ted?"

It surprises Ted, hearing this stranger say his name. Then Ted recognizes him, dressed in his familiar dark coveralls.

"Will? Is that you?"

"Yeah."

The gun is shaking in Ted's hands and he realizes he's still pointing it at Will. He clicks on the safety and lowers the gun before setting it on the chair.

"Jesus, Will! If you'd been at any other house on the bayou, you'd probably be dead right now."

"I'm glad I'm here, then," Will says.

"Please tell me it was Mr. Roy that sent you down here."

"I don't know what to say," Will says. Then he begins walking toward the street.

"Wait," Ted says and Will stops, but doesn't turn around. "Dammit, Will, of all people, why you? I mean, what would your Dad say if he knew what you were up to?"

Will still isn't saying anything.

"Well?"

"You don't understand, Ted. It's him that's making me do it."

"Oh," Ted says.

"I don't want to do it anymore," Will says, still with his back to Ted. "But I don't know how to make him stop."

"What are y'all doing with the ducks?"

"Eating them," Will says. He says it in a way that makes Ted feel foolish for asking. When Ted doesn't say anything, Will adds, "He's a good man, Ted, I swear. It's just that things haven't been too good for us this year. It's really changed him."

"You don't have to explain," Ted says.

They're both quiet. Then Will says, "I'm gonna go now, okay?"

"Wait," Ted says and he moves toward the pen. He starts to grab a mallard drake, a big greenhead, but then his hand is moving toward his father's hen, Susie. It's a good deal bigger than the greenhead. He takes the fat duck by the neck and lifts it flapping and kicking from the pen. "Here," Ted says.

Will hesitates.

"Just take it, okay?" Ted says. "It's important that you take it."

Will takes the duck by the neck. He says, "I better go now. My dad's waiting up the street."

"Okay," Ted says and he returns to the chair on the patio where he takes up the shotgun again. He doesn't let a minute pass before raising the gun, clicking off the safety, and aiming it over the pen of ducks and at the bayou. There's an explosion and a cloud of smoke. And then there is another explosion as he fires the second barrel. Again, the thunder rolls, roaring down the stillness of the bayou. Reaching beyond Mr. Bertrand's house a mile up river. Reaching also, Ted knows, anyone who might be parked on a street nearby. Now it's quiet.

Lights inside the house come on, first in the back and then in front. A moment later, a light next door at the Broussards' shows in the windows, and he knows everyone will be coming now, probably with their guns, wanting to see what happened, anxious to see the duck thief, whom, he will tell them, he saw, but somehow missed. They will be disappointed, but that doesn't matter. Tomorrow he will leave on an airplane and there will be no more ducks taken. Then things will return to normal—normal, at least, as the men up and down the bayou have come to see it.

{2}

A Changed Man

"Man, look at you!" Frank said. "So that's what a daddy looks like, uh." Frank stood at the front door with a gift bag and a twelve-pack of beer. Looking ridiculous, not because of the beer, but because the gift bag was small, pink, and had yellow tissue paper coming out the top of it. Frank wasn't the sort of person you'd ever associate with pink or yellow. People like him didn't show up at your door bearing gifts of any kind, unless you considered beer a gift.

"Hey, boy," Big John said. "What you know?" He took the beer from Frank and then shook his hand, the one not holding the gift bag. He looked down at Frank's work boots and hoped they weren't as filthy as they looked. Knowing they were because he wore them all the time.

"Mais, me, I don't know nuttin'. But I bet you do," Frank said, and he handed the gift bag to Big John like he couldn't get rid of it fast enough. "I had nuttin' to do with it," Frank said. "It was all Sheila's idea. I think it's some little clothes or somethin'."

"Thanks, podnah. Dorothy'll appreciate it," Big John said, looking as awkward holding the gift bag as Frank had.

Years ago, Frank and Big John had played football together in high school. Now they both worked at the rice mill in town. For some time now, they'd shared a lease in Pecan Island where they had a camp. They hunted ducks and deer and went redfishing a lot together.

"Sheila says she's sorry she couldn't make it," Frank said as he followed Big John through the door and then through the kitchen, looking around like it was his first time in the house. "You sure it's okay we can watch the Saints here? We ain't gonna wake the baby up or nuttin'? It'd do no good to piss off Dorothy."

"Nah, man, don't worry about it," Big John said. "I told her you were comin' by. Anyway, she's in back. I think she's feeding the baby or something."

Big John never was sure what his wife and the baby did back there. He always felt like he was intruding, like walking in on girls getting dressed. Even when his wife said she wanted him back there to help out or just to talk to the baby girl. She said the baby needed to get used to his voice, but he never knew what to say. Big John felt foolish talking to something that small, to a baby who couldn't possibly understand anything he was saying or respond if it could. When his wife was still pregnant, she made Big John talk to her swollen belly every night before turning out the lights for bed.

"Hey, Dorrie," Big John shouted down the hall, "Frank's here. We gonna be in the living room, okay?" He waited a few seconds in silence to see if his wife would say anything back, but she didn't. Then he put the gift bag on top of the TV cabinet before returning his attention to Frank. "They must be asleep," he said. "You want a beer?"

"Mais, hell yeah."

The game hadn't started yet, it wouldn't for a little while. Big John noticed Frank looking at the balloon they'd brought home from the hospital. It had risen to the ceiling and was metallic looking and colorful. It had a thin red ribbon tied to it that hung toward the floor in bouncy curlicues. In fat letters, the balloon announced: "It's a girl!"

Frank and Big John sat in the living room with their beers not saying anything, like there wasn't anything to say. Like things were so different now and there wasn't anything to talk about.

Frank was smaller than Big John, but was still tall and rangy. Unlike Big John, he was quick-tempered and just as quick to fight and fight dirty. You had to watch him. He wouldn't think twice about picking up a pipe or a brick or a beer bottle if within reach. On his belt, he wore a five-inch gutting-knife in a leather case. He kept the blade sharp and was always cleaning his fingernails with it, wanting everyone to see it. Big John looked at the knife on Frank's hip and wondered if Dorothy would allow it in the house now that there was a baby living there. Big John and his wife had already had a fight about all the shotguns and the deer rifle he had. He kept them in the gun cabinet in their bedroom. She said she wanted the guns out of the house, but he didn't have anywhere else to keep them.

Big John could tell Frank was going to say something about the balloon, probably make a wisecrack about it. Before he could Big John said, "So how's things at work?"

"You know, same old shit."

"I hear that," Big John said, yawning big. He knew nothing ever changed at the mill, but thought he'd ask anyway.

In the corner of the living room there was a little pink and green baby seat that reclined, vibrated, and played music when the baby was strapped into it. Big John saw Frank looking at it now. When Frank looked at Big John and noticed he was watching him he shook his head laughing. He said, "Man, first Douglas, now you. What's the world coming to, uh?"

Frank was referring to Douglas Premeaux, a co-worker at the mill whose wife had had a baby earlier that year. Big John shook his head and felt his face growing hot.

"So, c'mon, man, talk to me," Frank prodded. "What's being a daddy like?"

"I don't know," Big John said, and it was true, he didn't know. He still didn't know what to make of any of it. His wife had only had the baby earlier that week and Big John had taken off work to help out until his mother-in-law could take off time from her job at Landry's department store in town. It'd been six days and he was anxious to get back to the mill. He didn't like staying home the way he had thought he would have. He'd thought it was going to be more like a vacation. If he'd known beforehand that it was going to be the way it turned out, he wouldn't have ever asked for the time off.

Frank took a long gulp of his beer, which was the way he drank beer. He waited for Big John to continue. When Big John still hadn't said anything, Frank egged him on.

"Whatcha mean you don't know? It's a simple question, podnah. What the hell's it like? Are you a changed man or what? You gonna turn all soft like Douglas done?"

Big John knew what Frank really meant. From the moment he'd heard about the baby coming Frank was worried it would change everything. He said he'd seen it before. That having a baby was worse than getting married, even. That once the kids started popping out everything ended. All the partying. All the hunting and fishing. Everything. Now Frank had Douglas Premeaux to use as an example and he did every chance he got.

"No, I ain't changed," Big John said, yawning big again. "But I can say one thing, though: I don't get no sleep anymore. That's for damn sure. Baby's up all night crying—I don't think I got two hours sleep last night."

"Man, that ain't right," Frank said, crushing his beer can and burping at the same time. "Man needs his sleep."

"Yeah. But they say it's supposed to get better after a couple a months."

"You gonna be able to hunt for teal season?"

"I guess so."

"You guess so, uh. Opening day is only four weeks away. You do realize that?"

"Yeah, I realize that. I got a calendar."

Frank huffed through his nose.

Big John said, "Look, don't worry, man. Once I start work again tomorrow I'll be back into the old routine. You'll see. Things'll get back to normal."

"Well, I sure as hell hope so," Frank said. He'd gotten up and was now moving from the room. He continued talking and Big John could hear him in the kitchen. "Because if you can't hack it, man, I'll get someone else to take over your half the lease. Bertrand already says he's interested. So did Dale Guidry."

When Frank came back into the room Big John said "Why the hell are you in such a hurry to sell off my half? Hell, I put as much work into that camp as you did. It's half mine."

"Mais, it ain't like that, podnah," Frank said. He handed Big John a fresh beer before moving back to the recliner and falling into it heavily. Frank opened his beer and gulped down a third of it. Beer never lasted long with Frank around. Frank said, "I just don't want to be stuck paying for everything by myself, that's all."

"Damn, you think things have changed that much?" Big John said. His first beer was still half full and he put the new one on the floor next to his chair before continuing. "Christ, Frank. So my old lady had a baby. What's the big deal?"

Frank didn't say anything. He smiled like he wanted to say something, but he kept quiet with what was on his mind. Then he said, "See if the Saints are on yet."

"What channel?" Big John said, already flipping through the channels with the remote.

"I don't know. Try nine or eleven," Frank said as he pulled a cigarette and a lighter from his shirt pocket. He put the cigarette between his lips. Big John noticed before he could get it lit.

"Not in the house."

"What?"

"Because the baby," Big John said. "Dorothy's not letting anyone smoke in the house anymore."

"You're kidding."

"Nope."

"She ain't letting you smoke in your own house?"

"Nuhn-uhn."

She wasn't letting Big John wear shoes in the house anymore, either, but for a reason he couldn't figure. He still hadn't worked up the nerve to tell Frank to take off his work boots. If Dorothy came into the room and saw the boots, she'd tell him to take them off. That was a scene Big John was dreading.

Frank placed the cigarette behind his ear. He said, "Ain't that some shit."

Big John said, "It ain't good for the baby, so I smoke on the patio. It really ain't that big a deal, man."

"Guess she don't let you smoke pot in the house anymore, either?"

Big John didn't like the way Frank was making him feel.

"I knew it," Frank said. "See, it's already started."

Big John hated the way Frank said it, all that was implied by it. He said, "Man, shut the fuck up with all that, uh. I'm tired of it."

"All I'm saying is that it's changed everything."

"Stop saying that," Big John said. He hated that Frank kept saying it. But he hated more that it was true. Partly true, anyway, because while everything had changed—how could it not with a baby being born—he himself hadn't changed with it. At least not in the way he'd expected. In the way he'd hoped. Nothing was like he thought it would be.

The moment Douglas Premeaux at work had heard the news of Big John's baby coming, he'd gone on and on about it. About his own experience at the hospital. About what to expect. He constantly talked to Big John about the first time he'd held his baby daughter. How amazing it was. He said he envied Big John for the experience he was about to have. Douglas Premeaux said he'd cried. He swore he was a changed man and it was clear to everyone—Big John included—that Douglas Premeaux had indeed changed. Dale would sit with the men at lunch or at the coffee pot and Douglas Premeaux would say out of the blue, right in the middle of a conversation about football or getting pussy, how he wished he were at home holding his baby. Or how he couldn't wait to go home at night so he could feed her. Or rock her to sleep.

He'd say it in front of the other men and not care what they thought. It was hard to imagine someone like Douglas Premeaux acting like that. He was a big man, bigger than Big John even, a real tough son of a bitch. It was hard to imagine that he wouldn't crush something as fragile as an infant in his large, powerful arms.

But seeing the transformation in Douglas Premeaux had excited something in Big John. It had gotten so that Big John was eager for the change that was coming. Then when his baby girl was born and the change didn't come with it, he wasn't sure what to think. When the doctor pulled the baby out of his wife in the delivery room and then showed it to him, Big John thought it was the most alien-looking thing he'd ever seen. All red and slimy. Looking like a skinned nutria, he couldn't help thinking at the time.

Nothing clicked the way he had expected. It didn't feel natural holding the baby the way he thought it would even though it was his daughter, his own blood. And he knew he didn't look natural holding her, either. He'd seen pictures of himself, looking awkward, pained even, not looking anything like what Douglas Premeaux had described all those times. Yet, Big John was hopeful that the change was still coming, that it came to men at different times. That it would come to him, too, sooner or later, and he was waiting.

"Turn up the TV," Frank said, now sitting sideways in the recliner with his legs draped over the armrest. "The game's about to start."

Big John turned up the volume. Loud enough to placate Frank, but not so loud that it might piss off Dorothy. Big John didn't want to wake the baby. He didn't want his wife coming out now and seeing Frank's big, filthy boots. She would throw a fit.

Just then Big John heard something stir at the back of the house. Then the bedroom door opened and he could hear his wife making shushing noises as she moved down the hall toward the living room. Frank and Big John looked at each other like a couple of teenagers caught in the middle of something.

"Hey, Dorrie," Frank said in the funny voice he always used when talking to Big John's wife.

"Hey, yourself," Dorothy said, looking at the baby and not Frank, and Big John realized she wasn't coming to the living room because she was mad. She wasn't going to yell at him in front of Frank like he had thought.

Frank liked big tits. He was always talking about it at work. Big John could see Frank staring at his wife's breasts now, taking a long look, seeing that they were much bigger than normal, swollen with mother's milk. What Frank couldn't see beneath the fabric of her shirt were her nipples, the way they were mashed, mangled and bloody from the baby's ineptitude at nursing.

Dorothy said in a happy voice, "So, Frank, you ready to meet Patricia Olivia?"

Dorothy tilted her arms, presenting the baby girl who was swaddled tightly in a blanket and sound asleep.

"That's her name?" Frank said. He sounded surprised for some reason.

"Yeah, Patricia Olivia Boudreaux. What'd you think her name was?"

"I don't know. It's the first I heard it."

"John!" Now Dorothy was looking at Big John and not sounding happy anymore. "Mais, I can't believe! You didn't even tell him her name?"

"I don't know," Big John said. "I was going to. It just didn't never come up."

"God," Dorothy said. "I really wonder about you."

Now she was yelling at Big John in front of Frank the way he'd not wanted her to. He could tell Frank was enjoying it. For some reason, Big John found it difficult raising his voice in anger when the baby was around, even though his wife seemed to have no problem with it at all.

"C'mon, Dorrie, stop ridin' me, uh," Big John said. "Frank just got here. I was going to tell him. I wanted him to see her first, okay?"

"Yeah, right," Dorothy said. Now she was looking into the baby's face again and didn't seem angry anymore. "Anyway," Dorothy went on, "I need you to watch her while I make a run to the store. We're almost out a diapers again."

Big John sat up in the chair. He said, "I don't know, Dorrie. You think that's a good idea?"

"Well I'm not sending you again," she said to Big John. Then to Frank, "Last time he went he got diapers for a toddler and not a preemie."

Big John doubted Frank knew what exactly constituted a toddler—or a preemie, for that matter—but it was plain from the grin on Frank's face that he knew enough of what Dorothy was saying to know Big John had screwed up.

Dorothy pulled the burping cloth from under the baby's head and draped it over Big John's shoulder. Then she lowered the little baby girl toward him. Remembering best he could how to hold a baby, the way he'd learned in class, Big John took his daughter into his large hands, careful not to crush her, careful to support her head. Still, the baby came to rest a little too quickly onto his shoulder.

"John!" Dorothy snapped. "Be careful!"

"I'm trying," he said in a hushed tone. He didn't want to startle the baby. He didn't want to wake her up.

"If she wakes up," Dorothy said, "just walk her around the room some. That usually does the trick." Before Big John could say anything, Dorothy grabbed her purse, headed for the front door, and was gone.

Frank looked like he'd never seen a man holding a baby before, a look of wonder mixed with ridicule. Big John had muted the TV and it was quiet. Neither of them dared talk, not wanting to wake the baby.

Still, within five minutes, the baby began to stir. Then she was crying. It was a whimper at first, which quickly turned to an all out bawling. Big John could tell by Frank's face that he didn't know what to think. Big John did as his wife instructed. He walked around the room with the baby on his shoulder. He made shushing sounds, while gently patting her on the back.

"Damn, you wouldn't think something so little could make that much noise," Frank said after draining his beer and crushing the can. Big John was thinking the same thing, but didn't say.

Frank went to the kitchen for another beer and then was back in the TV room. "I think I'll go outside and have that smoke now," he said, and he exited the back door, leaving Big John alone with the baby.

It was times like this that had Big John wondering. This was his little girl, yet he didn't feel the connection that might have had him feeling love and not repulsion. 'It's different when it's your baby,' Douglas Premeaux had told him one day at the mill. 'You'll see. Don't worry about it.' Well, nothing was happening the way Douglas Premeaux said it would and Big John half-wondered if they'd mixed up the babies at the hospital. It happened on TV and in movies sometimes, so it was bound to happen in real life once in a while. He imagined another man somewhere across town holding a bawling baby girl and not feeling anything for it, unable to shut her up.

A moment later Frank came back inside. When ten more minutes had passed, and the baby was still crying, Big John was at a loss. He glanced at the digital clock on the VCR and couldn't believe his wife had only been gone that little bit of time.

"Damn it!" Big John said.

"You want me to try?" Frank said, sitting in the recliner again.

"Hell, I don't know," Big John said. Then, "You serious?"

Frank stood up, eager. "I don't know, why not?" he said. "I ain't never held no baby before. Maybe I got the touch."

"Hell, at this point I'll try anything," Big John said. As gently as he could, he handed the little screaming baby to Frank who held his rough, calloused hands open like a misshapen bowl. "Her little neck muscles ain't developed yet," Big John said, "so you're gonna want to support her head, okay?"

"Alright," Frank said, smiling a stupid grin, and he took the baby into his hands. Holding the baby out from his body, Frank studied her red, screaming, contorted face. "C'mon, you little thing. It's me, Frank. Me and your old man, we pod-nahs. C'mon now, stop your cryin', uh."

It surprised Big John to see Frank being nice, even to a little baby. Still, he didn't like watching Frank hold his daughter. Big John was sorry he'd handed her over. He wanted her back.

"Okay, that's good. I'll take her back now."

"C'mon, man, I just got her. I bet I can make her stop. Just give me a minute," Frank said. Then he was talking to the baby again, "So you're what's done it, uh? Mais, I never thought something as little as you could change someone as big as your old man."

Frank looked at Big John, smiling at the joke.

"Cut it out, man," Big John said. "Seriously, give her back."

"In a minute," Frank said, and the baby wasn't any closer to not crying. She sounded like she was in pain, even though Big John could see that Frank wasn't doing anything to hurt her. Then Frank was talking to the baby again, but still looking at Big John. "Not even your momma could do it, and, let me tell you, she was somethin'. But along you come and just like that he's hen-pecked. He's a ruined man."

"Goddammit, Frank, give her back, I mean it," Big John said. When he moved toward Frank and reached for the baby, Frank turned so that Big John couldn't get his hands on her. The baby continued crying.

"What's it like to have that kind of power over a man, uh?"

Frank continued. "Oh, but just you wait. In fifteen years or so you'll have that same power only it'll be over some poor young hard leg who's burning to get inside your little panties."

Big John was getting mad. He would have punched Frank square in the jaw if he'd not been holding his baby. Big John thought about punching him anyway. When Frank turned back toward him, Big John lunged forward and put both his hands around the baby. Frank resisted at first and the baby was momentarily caught in a tug-of-war. She shrieked inhuman-like and Frank let go. Then Big John had the baby in his arms again.

"Sonofabitch!" Frank said, looking scared. "You crazy?"

Big John was so mad he had tears in his eyes. "Get the fuck out my house!"

Frank didn't say anything. He stood there considering Big John; not looking scared anymore, just incredulous. Big John kept an eye on Frank's hands, on the gutting knife at his hip.

Frank said, "What the hell I want to stay here for anyway?" Frank made a wide arc out of the room, before moving toward the front door. The whole time keeping an eye on Big John, as if he might decide to come at him. Even with the baby in his arms. Then the door slammed shut, making a terrific noise. But it didn't matter because the baby was already awake and crying. She was still bawling and Big John wondered if she was okay. She was so tiny, so fragile, and he hoped she was all right.

"It's okay, you little thing," he said in a voice that came out calmer than anything he'd ever heard come from his own mouth. "It's okay, Boo. Daddy's got you." The baby continued crying, but it was okay now. She was safe. "Everything's going to be all right. I'm here now. Daddy's here."

Big John wasn't sure, but he might have felt for a second like a father and liked it. The baby was still crying hysterically, her face still red and twisted, but now everything was okay. It was his baby, his little girl, his daughter, and everything was all right. He made shushing noises the way his wife did when trying to calm down the baby. He rocked her gently, still making the shushing noises, wondering what was taking his wife so long.

{3}

Voyeurs

Kent woke up and was thirsty. Marcie lay buried beneath the covers sound asleep. Not wanting to wake her, he rolled carefully out of bed before padding barefoot to the kitchen. He tried making himself as light as possible on the old hardwoods. Even then, the floor creaked and whined under each step.

In the kitchen, he filled a glass from the tap. He sat at the table before pulling a cigarette from the pack that was next to the ashtray, a large, gaudy ceramic replica of the Lincoln Memorial they'd bought their first week in the city, when still feeling like tourists.

When Kent looked up, he noticed a girl in the window of the building nextdoor; directly across the alley from their apartment, also four floors up. She was in a bedroom changing out of what looked like a charcoal-gray business suit. Behind her, the two doors of a wide closet were open, revealing a long rod of hanging clothes. Now in a slip, the girl appeared to be browsing the closet for another outfit. She looked like Kent sometimes might when standing for a long time before the open refrigerator, not searching for anything in particular. He glanced at the digital clock on the microwave. It was

31

after 2 a.m.

The girl wasn't exactly a looker. At least Kent didn't think so. She had long, silky blond hair, and he liked that. But she appeared tall, thin, and boney in the slip. The way models look awkward and ungainly when not wearing the kinds of clothes that can suddenly transform them into something stunning to behold. It disappointed him to realize he'd found the girl more attractive when fully-dressed. Still, there she was, and he found something curious about her, about the fact that she didn't know someone was watching her. Next, the girl tried on a black, floor length gown, and then a burgundy cocktail dress, both times checking herself out in the window that was apparently like a mirror in the brightly lighted room against the darkness of the night outside. She turned this way and that, making faces that Kent recognized as disapproval.

He didn't know what she was doing, there were no hints in her actions, so he couldn't help making up stories about her. He figured she had an important interview the next day, maybe on Capitol Hill. Or maybe she had a date with someone she really liked and she wanted to make a good impression. A first date, perhaps. The changing and unchanging went on for over an hour before she stopped, not seeming to have resolved anything. She simply closed the closet doors and turned off the overhead light, before moving to a bed that was partially visible through a second window. She turned off another light and then it was dark. Unable to see anything anymore, Kent felt foolish, sitting in the dark kitchen in the middle of the night.

The next night Kent and Marcie were in bed. As usual,

Marcie fell asleep first, around midnight. Kent lay positioned behind her, feeling the warmth pouring through her silk nightgown. Two hours later, and unable to sleep, he watched the illuminated numbers of the digital clock. The girl from the night before was on his mind and he wondered if she might be up. She probably wouldn't be, he thought. But what if she were? He rolled out of bed as quietly as he could and then made his way to the kitchen, feeling like a teenager again, prowling around his parents' house in the dark. As he entered the kitchen Kent saw the girl in the window across the alley. He pulled a cigarette from the pack, lit it, and made himself comfortable at the table. Like he was in a jazz bar or a strip club and not a kitchen.

Just as the night before, the girl wore a white slip and was trying on outfits. Kent wondered if she had a second interview? Did she have another date with her dream guy? Now she tried on a green plaid skirt, studying herself in the window as she buttoned the cuffs of a starched white blouse. She looked like an anorexic schoolgirl. Then she stopped for a moment, frozen. Kent, too, remained motionless as the girl appeared to be looking out the window and not into it anymore. She seemed to be looking directly at him and Kent wondered if she could see him sitting there in the kitchen. But he knew she couldn't see him as long as the kitchen light was off. He kept the cigarette behind the large ashtray and out of sight. A moment later, the girl continued posing in the window before taking off the outfit. After carefully putting the clothes back on hangers, she returned them to the long rod in the closet.

Like the night before, she tried on several more outfits and then seemed content to go to bed, turning off the lights and sending Kent to the bedroom where he resumed his place next to his wife.

———

Kent wondered if it had become an obsession. He knew it had become a routine; quietly rolling out of bed around two o'clock every morning and then going to the kitchen where he'd sit smoking while watching the girl undress and then dress before undressing again.

He sat in the kitchen now, smoking his fourth cigarette. That's when he heard the floorboards creaking and he knew Marcie was up. As she entered the kitchen, she turned on the light. Kent knew the girl across the alley could see him now.

"What are you doing?" Marcie said.

"I couldn't sleep, so I decided to smoke a cigarette." He took a drag and blew out the smoke, as if to prove it.

"In the dark?"

"Since when do you need the lights on to smoke?"

"Just seems a little strange, that's all," she said, yawning. She moved to the refrigerator, opened the door, and looked inside.

"Want something to eat?" he said. "I could make you an egg. Or a sandwich." After pausing, he added, "How 'bout an egg sandwich?" Kent chuckled, wondering if Marcie had picked up on the word play.

She either didn't hear him or else didn't think it was funny, because she wasn't laughing when she closed the refrigerator door. She stood behind him, not saying anything. Then she said, "Oh my God, look at that girl."

"Where?" Kent said, pretending to look everywhere but at the only lighted window among the hundreds they could see from their kitchen.

"Right there," Marcie said. "Are you blind?"

The overhead light had turned the kitchen window into a mirror and Kent could clearly see himself in the reflection seated at the table, and Marcie standing behind him. Beyond that he could just make out the girl, now appraising herself in her own window, turning her hips and checking out her butt, the usual look of disapproval.

"She probably doesn't realize anyone can see her since all she can see is herself in the reflection of her window," Kent said, sounding like he'd put some thought into it. He hoped it didn't sound like it to Marcie.

"God, you are naïve," Marcie said, now talking in the tone she used when belittling him. "Believe me, she knows what she's doing. She's an exhibitionist. I mean look at her."

Kent mashed out his cigarette in the ashtray. He resisted the urge to speak in the girl's defense. "Well, anyway, I've had my cigarette," he said, rising from the table. "You can stay if you want, but I'm going back to bed."

Kent was impressed with his performance, his quick improvisation. Marcie didn't seem to suspect a thing. He knew he would've known it if she did. She would have let him know it.

"Suit yourself," Marcie said.

When Kent turned around he was surprised to see Marcie now seated at the table, pulling a cigarette from the pack.

"Now I'm not sleepy," she said, lighting the cigarette. "Turn the light off before you go, okay?"

———

Kent wondered how long it'd been going on. How long had this girl been doing this, right there in plain view? Did it happen every night? What else was he oblivious to? What else went on in the windows outside their apartment? He'd never thought about it before. He'd never had a reason to.

Nevertheless, he saw the girl differently now. After Marcie

had labeled her an exhibitionist, the act of spying on her felt different. It didn't seem so innocent anymore. He wondered if going to the kitchen every night had become more than just a curiosity the way it was in the beginning. Could one person's fetish unwittingly draw out someone else's latent obsession? Had he been a closet-voyeur all along in need of an exhibitionist to bring it to the surface? It was crazy thinking like that, he thought, but there was little else to do but think while waiting in the dark. He'd got to the kitchen earlier than usual, about one o'clock, and the windows of the apartment across the alley were dark. As he sipped from his third bottle of beer, he looked out at all the windows of the apartment building across the alley, at the hundreds of windows of all the other apartment buildings beyond that. He wondered how many other people were sitting patiently in the dark like he was now, waiting. He didn't want to think of himself like that and decided he'd give the girl a few more minutes before going to bed. He'd finish his cigarette and then call it a night.

Then, as the light switched on in the window across the alley, Kent quickly mashed out the cigarette in the ashtray. The girl entered the room, seeming to come in from a night out. She casually tossed her purse onto a chair and took off her coat. Without pause, and in the manner of someone thinking they're not being watched, she began removing her clothes, kicking off her jeans, and working her way out of a long-sleeve shirt. As she stood there in her closet, wearing purple lace panties and a matching bra, Kent found it a little disconcerting. She'd always worn a slip before and he was used to it. He felt like he was watching a different girl altogether.

A moment later, Kent heard the footsteps coming from the back of the apartment, coming quickly, and he knew he was busted. The kitchen light came on.

"So this is it, huh?" Marcie said. "This is what you do every night?"

"No," he said.

"You're sick, Kent. You know that? Your wife's in bed, and you're over here watching little miss anorexic skank prancing in the window."

"It's not like that and you know it, Marcie."

"Then how is it? I mean you're sitting here every night watching this girl."

Kent didn't like how it sounded. He pulled another cigarette from the pack and lit it. He didn't know if Marcie knew for a fact that he'd been doing it every night or if she only suspected it. He didn't know what to say.

"Well?" she said.

"Well, what?"

"What are you doing, that's what?" she said. "How long's it been going on? Weeks? Months? The whole time we've been here?"

"No."

"You still haven't answered me. What are you doing here in the dark? You getting off on it? You like playing with yourself in the kitchen every night?"

"That's so stupid," he said. "You would think that."

In the reflection of the window, Kent could see Marcie standing behind him. He wanted to tell her it'd only been going on for about two weeks. But he knew in the context of the argument it would do little to improve his position.

"I've just gotten in the habit of smoking a cigarette or two in the middle of the night," he said. "That's all."

"And drinking," she said.

"Big deal, so maybe I have a beer once in a blue moon," he said. He hoped she wouldn't check the garbage can under the sink where he'd thrown the two empties. "I can't help it if I have insomnia. I don't want to wake you up, so I come out here to smoke a cigarette. And, yes, to maybe have a beer if I feel like it. So what?"

"How lucky for you, the way your insomnia happens to co-incide with the nightly strip tease."

"Actually, she just came home, Marcie, so you obviously don't know what you're talking about. She wasn't even there until a few minutes ago." Kent thought that proved some-thing, but Marcie didn't seem to think it proved anything. Now that he'd said it, he didn't think it really proved any-thing either.

He could tell Marcie was angry now. It took a lot to get her mad. And, once mad, it took just as long to calm her down. When he'd not turned to face her, she moved in front of him and now stood there, her arms crossed. When he didn't say anything, she continued ranting, getting madder. Kent knew it still wasn't as bad as it was going to get. She was just getting started.

He sat there taking it, and as her rage escalated he realized he wasn't feeling shame. At least not the kind of shame he might have once expected to feel. He felt something else, something more akin to embarrassment than regret. He had the urge to hide, to turn off the light, he had the feeling of suddenly being put on display.

{4}

All That Remained

It was some time after midnight and the cattle stood bunched together at the highest point on the big levee. The eye of the hurricane had slammed into the coast not far to the west, stalled, then continued landward. Now the storm was picking up speed and the wind raged violently around the cattle, pelting their backsides with sand, horizontal rain, and cutting bits of debris. They knew something was coming, not knowing what exactly, but aware of something and knowing that it was better being exposed at the top of the big levee and not in the pasture below where there was a marked windbreak.

Not long after the storm made landfall, the eye-wall pushed the first mountainous wave toward the levee. The water level, ten to fifteen feet below the levee a moment earlier, all at once topped the bank and then the cattle were standing in warm salt water. The mother cows called frantically to the calves that were suddenly drawing on their instinct to swim, and the waves continued rolling at them. Each successive wave hitting them higher and harder than the one before until the water was breaking over their backs. The cattle in the pastures below were carried off into the darkness, along with everything else that could float or be pushed by the force of the oncoming rush of seawater.

An older cow, a Charolais with a blue numbered ear tag, instinctively moved through the water toward the east levee. The big levee had served its purpose and now she sensed they needed to get off it and back toward the front of the property while there was still time. She moved and the others followed her. She led them to the narrow levee and felt her way onto it. It was slow going. There was no room for error; a deep canal flanked one side, the flooded pasture the other. She continued on and the others followed, moving single file through the water. They were all going to make it off the big levee.

Maybe twenty-five of them were already on the narrow east levee when the next big wave came rolling toward them. It carried with it a terrifying noise, and then something was crashing over the big levee. Something large and it was there, instantly crushing three calves and a cow under its tremendous weight. The night was dark, but the thing was enormous, and so was the space it filled, its silhouette darker than the night around them. Those remaining could no longer follow the line of cattle making their way onto the east levee.

The cattle still on the big levee reluctantly backed away from the large grinding and creaking thing, and waited for it to move. Fighting the water that pushed and then pulled at them, keeping as much contact as possible between their hooves and the ground that at times didn't seem to be there in the rising and falling water. But the thing appeared anchored now, rocking and moaning and still groaning hideously, and the cattle backed away. They were stranded on the big levee and they waited as the storm continued to intensify. It was only the beginning, but they couldn't have known that.

As he had done a thousand times before, Lester LaPierre drove to the farm. His son, Ted, was already out there feeding and watering the cattle. Almost a week after the hurricane, the herd was still in desperate shape. Many of the cattle were still missing. Earlier that morning Ted had helped Junius Dugas, their tenant rancher, unload a flatbed trailer stacked high with hay bales that had come in from Texas. They were situating the bales in the barn when they heard the horn honk. Ted took off his hat, wiped his face with the sweat-soaked sleeve of his T-shirt, and looked toward the gate. His father sat in the truck waiting for him to come over and let him into the barnyard.

"I'm gonna ride with him to the back to see if there are any cattle still on the big levee," Ted said to Junius Dugas, a taciturn man who had been even more quiet than usual. He was in his sixties, was small and wiry, and had had close to a hundred head of cattle out on the farm before the storm. Many with calves. He still hadn't found a lot of them and that seemed to weigh heavily on his mind. And that was when he wasn't thinking about his house, which had flooded and was now left with six inches of mud in it. Like his son's house and his daughter's house and the houses of almost everyone he knew, it was a total loss and would need to be gutted down to the framework if he hoped to salvage at least that.

"Wanna take a ride?" Ted asked Junius Dugas.

"No, you go 'head. Go see what you can see," he said, not stopping in his work. He hefted a sixty pound hay bale and then threw it to the top of the stack. The way he'd been doing all that morning. The way Ted had had a hard time doing even when fresh and not fatigued the way he was now.

Ted's rubber boots offered little traction and, as if on ice, he half-walked and half-ran toward the gate. He was careful not to slip and fall in the thick sludge that was slow to dry in the shadows of the barnyard. He knew he had to keep an eye out for the many nails that were sticking out of the planks and plywood that lay scattered in piles everywhere. After letting his father into the barnyard, Ted swung the heavy gate shut before walking around to the passenger side. Before getting into the truck he let out the dog so it could run alongside as they drove toward the back of the property. Ted's knee boots were caked thick with mud and hay. There was little he could do to clean them off, so he didn't bother doing anything and got into the truck.

Ted's father rolled down his window, but left the air conditioner on. Ted didn't roll down his window. He adjusted the vent so he could feel the cool air through the wet, gritty T-shirt that clung heavily to his stomach.

"It's hot, uh?" his father said, handing Ted a bottle of water. Ted didn't say anything. He knew his father already knew it was hot. "What about Junius?" his father added. "He got anything to drink?"

"Yeah, the water came back on this morning. We've been drinking from the hose."

His father nodded. "No more trips to town, uh. Mais, you gotta be happy about that."

Until that morning, they'd had to haul tanks of water in from the water works plant in Abbeville twice a day. A twenty-five-mile round trip.

Ted's attention was now on the bottle of water. He couldn't get it open fast enough. He tipped the bottle so that the cold water poured into his mouth faster than he could swallow it. It spilled down his face and neck and onto his wet T-shirt. Out of breath, Ted lowered the bottle nearly empty. He thought about pouring what was left on his head.

"The power back on in town?" Ted asked.

His father shook his head. Air conditioners in cars and trucks were all the air conditioning there was. Everyone found excuses to go places so they could sit in the cool air. Ted dreaded the nights and having to sleep in the stifling heat, able to sleep only because he was so exhausted from the day's work.

Ted's father handed him a five-pound link of summer sausage, knowing he needed the salt as much as the protein. Ted was hungry and he quickly cut off a large piece of the sausage with his pocketknife. He looked out the window and took in the spectacle of the barnyard. It was still hard to believe. The tidal surge had come ashore, moving inland as far as the barn, and then three miles beyond that. It had deposited layer upon layer of debris all over the property.

People were riding around looking for their belongings. One couple driving by in a pickup was happy to find their wicker sofa, gaudy looking with its bright yellow and teal floral cushions. It had somehow turned up in one of the holding pens behind the barn. As they slowly drove by, Ted had noticed the two matching chairs in the back of the pickup. He'd waved down the people and they stopped. As Ted helped the man carry the sofa out of the pen, many times its normal weight because of the mud-soaked cushions, the man went on about how lucky they were to find the furniture, the entire set. As if it were a miracle. Their house was gone and this furniture was all they had left now. Ted was made to feel good about that. Seeing how happy they were to find their complete set of cheap wicker furniture.

———

Ted had been to the farm everyday since the storm and still

couldn't get used to it. What had taken his grandfather and then his father sixty years to build was all wiped out in the span of a single night. It didn't seem fair.

The pickup moved down the narrow passage made by the bulldozer they'd borrowed. To clear a path through the heaps of wreckage, the bulldozer had pushed aside the ripped up lumber and marsh grass, oil drums and kids' toys, parts of houses, sheets of corrugated tin and uprooted trees; a 15-foot bass boat with its motor still locked in an upright position the way it'd been left at a dock somewhere. You couldn't lift a piece of plywood without stirring a twisted pile of cotton-mouths, displaced by the storm and seeming more pissed off than usual about it. There were fire ants everywhere and on everything. There were spiders.

The truck rolled slowly through the cattle in the barnyard that gravitated to the road where the ground was level and free of rubble. They blocked the way, looking lost, dazed, and in no hurry to move. After a while, the truck finally crossed a cattle guard into the front pasture.

The grass in the pastures had to be dead. The layer of salt-water-sludge that had been left by the receding water smothered everything now. The large round hay bales scattered randomly throughout the farm looked okay, but they were no good. Having sat for days in salt water, they now rotted from the inside out. They were getting moldier by the hour in the damp heat. Ted and Junius Dugas would have to move the hay off the farm because the cattle were still eating it. They had to eat something and, for a time, the decomposing hay was all there was. The cattle still hadn't grown accustomed to eating the feed and fresh hay that Ted and Junius Dugas were putting out for them.

It was hot, hotter than usual it seemed, and humid. And because of all the stagnant water everywhere the mosquitoes were out in swarms and ravenous. There were flies every-where, feasting on everything dead. It hadn't rained since the hurricane and it was needed badly now to saturate the pas-tures. To dilute the salt content left by the flood before it set in for good. The ground was drying. The four-inch layer of sludge, now sun-baked in the open pastures, was cracked the way it might be on a salt flat somewhere far away where there were no hurricanes.

The truck crawled through the front pasture, traveling along a fence line that slanted sharply under the burden of ev-erything it had caught in the surge. They passed all the feed stations Ted and Junius Dugas had laid out for the cattle—barrel halves and plastic tubs, anything that could hold pro-tein pellets. They'd moved the large circular hay pens from around the farm so that they were now concentrated in this one area, where they could be continually refilled with the fresh hay being trucked in from north Louisiana and Texas. There were tanks of fresh water there, also, that the cattle were finally finding. The herd was no longer drinking the water from the ditches and back pastures that would remain filled with salt water until they had a chance to fix the tractor that was needed to pump the farm dry. The water had risen high enough to submerge the tractor's engine block and now new parts were needed. And parts like that, plentiful only a week earlier, were hard to come across. Everyone needed them now.

Still chewing on a mouthful of sausage, Ted cut off another piece and put it into his mouth with the blade of his knife. And then, just like that, it occurred to him that the farm was all his father had had left.

"I can't believe you're getting rid of the cattle," Ted said, not looking at his father, but at a wooden coffee table outside his window. Just sitting there in the pasture as if it belonged.

His father didn't say anything.

The cattle were beginning to lose weight. Their ribs were starting to show. Many had calves and were still nursing. His parents had decided only the day before to sell off what was left of the herd. It was the only thing to do. Ted had come home the day after the storm and had spent twelve-and four-teen-hour days out there, helping Junius Dugas to water and feed the cattle. It would be that way for a long time. Long after Ted went back to Dallas. Anything they planted would die. There would be no winter grass that year. There would be no hay. The pastures wouldn't be ready to graze for another year. And maybe not by then, no one knew. There was no precedent for this kind of thing. The only safe bet would be to sell off the cattle while they still had some weight on them. Take a hit. Hopefully break even. It was okay, though, seeing how when they'd first gone out to the farm the day after the water began receding they'd not expected to find anything alive. How could anything have survived it? Then many of the cattle they did find on the property were someone else's. The cattle were traumatized and had a spooked look about them that told you they'd been through one hell of an ordeal. When the waves came ashore they had, in effect, lifted everything—whole herds of cattle included. Then after being carried inland for several miles, everything was deposited as the waves moved back out to sea. Most of their cattle, at least the cattle they'd managed to find so far, were in Delcambre. That was two miles away. The cattle now on the farm belonged, in large part, to families a mile or so to the south—the hides of their bellies, like the hides and bellies of their own cattle in town, raw and torn from being carried through trees and over brush and the many barbed wire fence lines.

Just then Ted noticed another dead horse, this one up against the fence line along with everything else the water had managed to trap there—more lumber, huge tree limbs, a ping pong table, all variety of household garbage; even a paddle boat, the kind you might see at a lake house on a Saturday afternoon. The horse, an old buckskin, was grossly inflated and ready to burst. Its stench would reach the barnyard, along with the odor of all the other dead and bloated horses that were around the place, hung up on fence lines or up against trees. It would be some time before Luke and Junius Dugas got around to burning all the rotting carcasses.

"How come most of the cattle seemed to make out, but the horses didn't?" Ted asked his father, breaking a silence that would have lasted an hour had he not spoken.

"They don't float," his father said, not bothering to look at the horse. He'd already seen enough dead horses.

"What do you mean they don't float?"

"I mean they don't float," his father said. "Not like a cow, they don't."

Ted said, "I thought horses were strong swimmers."

"I didn't say they couldn't swim. I said they don't float. You can swim around all you want, but if you don't find something to stand on after while, you're going to sink, and that's all there is to it. Unless you're full of gas, like a cow."

Ted wasn't sure. Still, he figured it made sense.

———

First it was golf that went. Because of his arthritis. Suddenly, and for the first time in his life, Ted's father could no longer swing a golf club. Once a scratch golfer, he had to swallow his pride and quit. Still, he kept his membership at the club so he could play cards and dominoes. He still had that, so long as his regular crowd didn't die off the way he said they'd already begun to.

Then it was hunting that went when it had become too difficult for him to walk in the marsh. But he still had fishing and he went redfishing in Pecan Island every day of the season for a while. That lasted a few years. Then the arthritis moved to his hips and knees so he could no longer get into and out of a boat at the dock. And that was the end of fishing.

And with each activity that was taken away from Ted's father, it was taken away from Ted. Because those were the things he'd done with his father when growing up. Those were the things they did together when he came home to visit.

Through it all, though, they'd always had the farm. When Ted came home to visit they would make at least one daily trip out there to ride the pastures. Usually first thing in the morning with cups of coffee and cigars. If nothing else, the farm would always be there. It was his grandfather's place just as it would be Ted's one day when his father died. They would always have that, because it didn't entail walking knee-deep in a marsh. There were no boats to step into or climb out of at a dock. It didn't require swinging a golf club. All it took was driving a pickup through a pasture and looking at cattle. So when everything else died, the farm was all that remained and it was a consolation they could both live with. It still offered them the venue needed to be alone together, to visit in silence or in conversation. Now that would be taken away like everything else. All that remained was gone and now there was nothing left.

———

The truck crossed the second cattle guard and entered into another pasture. The dog, after carefully negotiating the slick rails of the cattle guard, took off and was running into the pasture. A cow, with two calves in tow, kept a wary eye on the dog. The tall gray Brahma lowered her downward curving horns, indicating a defensive posture. When the cow took off after the dog, the dog appeared stunned. It wasn't used to having cows chase her. But this cow wasn't one of theirs and apparently wasn't used to yellow labs running through the pasture. The cow continued after the dog with a wild look in her eyes, the way she might take off after a coyote. She would have killed the dog had she been able to run it down, just like she would've had it been a coyote.

"Jolie!" Ted's father shouted at the dog.

"Crazy damn cow," Ted said, amazed at the speed with which an animal that large could move, and with such malice.

"Goddamn that Cecil Breaux," Ted's father said.

"That one of his?" Ted said, knowing who Cecil Breaux was. He had a herd of Brahma on the other side of the Delcambre Canal.

"Yeah. I told him he had some of his cows over here and he still hasn't come to get 'em."

Ted and Junius Dugas had been busting their asses out there all week and it didn't sit well with either of them that they were doing it for someone else's cattle. People were in no hurry to pick up cattle that they knew were being cared for better than they themselves could manage. Not when they had other cattle to find and hay and feed and water to round up. Not when they were having to deal with homes that, until a few days earlier, had been half submerged in seawater. Ted's father had told Cecil Breaux and the others whose cattle were on the farm that he wouldn't feed or water them anymore if they didn't come get them. But Ted's father wasn't like that and everyone knew it.

Slowly it had gotten so there was no reason to move back. That's what Ted had thought about while driving his parents back home. For the first time in their lives, his parents had evacuated for a hurricane. At the last minute, they'd driven to Dallas to wait out the storm.

On the long drive home, they sat silent with their own thoughts, as though reserving anything that could be said until they'd assessed the damage left by the storm. It was in this silence that it first occurred to Ted that he would never live in his hometown again. Of course, it's not like he ever would have moved back. There was little work in his field there, there were no advertising agencies in Abbeville, Louisiana. And he was by no means a rancher, so could never consider running a place like the farm. But it had somehow been enough to think that he might move back one day. He could always dream. His parents had moved back after his father retired from the oil business, so it always seemed plausible that he could do it, too. Friends he'd grown up with in the small town, and who were now living in other parts of the country, often talked about moving back. They talked of seeing their kids grow up together the way they had; of hunting and fishing and crawfish boils and immersed in the heritage that was there and not in Texas or California or anywhere else. Then twenty-five years went by and Ted realized that once his parents were dead, there would be nothing left to go back to. The house where he grew up would cease being his home when his parents were no longer living in it. Someone else would live there then, as hard as that was to fathom. He might never return to the farm once his father was gone. There would be no reason to. It was a hell of a thing to consider.

———

At the back of the property they approached the main pasture, a vast six-hundred-acre expanse that still lay under water and would remain flooded until the tractor was fixed. Even then it could take weeks to drain. Beyond the pasture, about a mile back, was the big levee that had been topped by a tidal surge for the first time in fifty years. His father stopped the truck at the water's edge and killed the motor. No longer feeling the air conditioning, Ted rolled down his window. The breeze in the open pasture felt good, almost cool in the heat and humidity. It smelled clean and wasn't stinking of rotting vegetation, sludge, and dead horseflesh.

A line of roseate spoonbills moved in the shallow water at the edge of the pasture, feeding on grass shrimp. In the distance, pelicans, ibis, and cormorants worked the water in tight groups. Sitting half-submerged at the center of the pasture was a small two-story house. Ted recognized it as L. D. Robichaux's hunting camp. Until a week ago, it had been sitting atop ten-foot creosote pylons, about a half-mile to the south, just shy of the bay. Now here it was, sitting in their back pasture. Aside from that, the house didn't seem wrecked in any way. It was as if someone might walk out of the door and onto the upstairs porch and wave at them.

Ted glanced at his father, who took a long puff of his cigar, seeming to chew the smoke. "Son of a bitch," he said.

"You still feeling up to it?" Ted said.

"Aren't you curious?"

"Yeah. But I can go alone if you want."

"It shouldn't be too hard if we keep to the levee," his father said. "It's under water, but it shouldn't be too deep. And I'll have my cane."

"Okay, then," Ted said, knowing he could never talk his father out of doing what he'd already set his mind to.

They hoped to find the rest of the herd. They were still missing fifty or sixty head, even after searching town and the neighboring ranches. If these cattle were out there, they'd have to be pushed to the barnyard. They would be in dire need of fresh water and feed.

Ted and his father put on their waders. Then they made their way toward the west levee, wading in waste-deep water. The walking was much easier once they'd climbed up the narrow levee, where the salt water was clear and well below their knees. Ted saw his father dip his finger into the water before tasting it on his tongue.

"Salty?" Ted asked, thinking the water looked fresh.

"As salty as the gulf."

The dog, no longer chasing after the spoonbills, was on the levee now. She ran past them, running without a purpose, running out of sheer excitement.

"Would you look at that," his father said, not pointing his cane at the dog, but instead at a spot where the levee dropped off into the pasture. It was a stingray, not a big stingray, but still an anomaly in the pasture. There had been stories of rice farmers outside of town finding four- and five-foot sharks in their fields, carried in with the tidal waves, now three miles inland.

"You could always keep some of the cattle," Ted said to his father as they continued walking. The old man had been quiet. "Keep fifty head," Ted added. "Or twenty five."

He knew his father came out to ride the pastures every morning around eight. He knew his mother went with him on Saturdays. It was firmly entrenched in their routine and they did it rain or shine. It was one of the few things they did together. Now they were talking about giving it up.

"What's the use?" his father said.

"Just so you'll have something to do. Everyone needs a purpose."

"You know, we never made a profit all these years. It's just been an expensive hobby. Your mother and me figured it's time to stop spending money. We can lease the land. Hell, it'll be nice to finally make money for a change."

"So what'll you do now? I can't see you just sitting around the house all day."

"We'll find something. We always do."

After about a mile, they finally reached the big levee. Now they walked along its broad flat ridge. Up above everything it was windy and it felt good.

"You can see how high the water got," his father said. He pointed at the bushes and trees growing along the edge of the bank where the levee dropped off some ten to fifteen feet into the Delcambre Canal. There was marsh grass and trash hung up in the branches at the tops of the trees. "The white caps would've been well over our heads," his father said.

"I can't believe the water came in that high."

"Can you imagine what those poor cows went through?" his father said. "When the first wave came ashore it was about two a.m., as black as coffee." They both studied the trodden ground, the sun-baked cloven hoof-prints where they were now standing, where the herd was standing when the surge came rushing over the levee. "Those poor old sons of bitches. I could just cry thinking about it."

"Think we'll find any still alive?"

"I don't think so. Not after seeing this."

Ted looked to the south and tried to imagine a wave of water coming at them. To give it perspective, he looked at the trash hung up in the tree branches above his head, a plastic grocery bag popping loudly in the wind, looking like some battle-tattered flag.

"Well, let's keep going. Maybe they'll surprise us," his father said, not sounding like he expected any surprises.

They moved toward a dense thicket of bamboo that had somehow withstood all the wind and water. They followed a narrow, winding path through the brush, which, over the years, had been worn deep into the levee by the cattle. Keeping an eye out for cottonmouths, Ted stepped on a limb that crossed the cow path, snapping it so his father could pass without having to step over it. As the crack of the limb shot out into the stillness, they heard a cow moo. Then there were more cows mooing.

"I'll be damned," his father said.

"How many do you think there are?"

"Let's go see," his father said, and they picked up the pace. Once out of the bamboo they could see the herd, what looked like thirty or forty in all. Some with calves. The cattle looked entranced, their long-lashed eyelids heavy with exhaustion. A few appeared spooked, showing the whites of their eyes in a peculiar way that warned Ted and his father that they had to be careful in the way they approached.

"Hold on a second," Ted's father whispered. "Let 'em take us in for a minute."

Behind the herd and blocking the narrow levee that ran along the east side of the property line was an enormous shrimp boat. At least a sixty-footer. The cattle stood their ground, facing Ted and his father with their backs to the boat. Ted and his father were careful not to make any sudden moves, not wanting the herd to feel cornered. All it would take is for one cow to make a run at them in a rush to get past, and then the whole herd would be stampeding.

Ted couldn't take his eyes off the shrimp boat. Shrimp boats were big, and wide-bodied. Out of the water, this one looked monstrous. Its deep-sea hull raised and sitting awkwardly on the small ridge, the boat listed to one side, exposing its barnacle littered belly and the long drive shafts leading to the two big propellers. Its pair of towering booms had collapsed and were now bent and sprawling about the ground. Ted noticed the brown and white hide and tail before realizing a cow had been crushed beneath the boat.

"There's the problem right there," Ted's father whispered.

"What?"

"The boat. It's blocking their way onto the east levee. That's how the rest of the herd got out. Single file, all the way down the levee. Can you imagine that? It took a lead cow to figure it out. And once she'd done it, the rest followed until this boat came ashore and blocked the way."

Those stranded on the big levee had been left most vulnerable to the wind. Ted noticed their tails swatting futilely at the swarms of biting flies that covered their backs and the open cuts and slashes inflicted by windborne objects. They looked like they'd been flogged.

"So why didn't they just turn around and go to the west levee? Hell, it's wider than this one."

"The lead cow was already gone. They were confused. Once they got it in their heads that this was the way to go, it's all they could think. Now they're hungry, thirsty, and exhausted and probably aren't thinking at all."

"So what now?"

"We push 'em back to the front."

"You sure about that?" Ted said, keeping an eye on a big crazed-looking cow that had some Brahma in her. "We could get Junius to help. He could probably borrow a horse somewhere."

"That won't be necessary."

"I don't know, dad. Look at thirty-four," Ted said, referencing the Brahma's numbered ear tag. "She's really spooked."

His father said, "She's just worried about her calf. They all are. But they're okay. Just a little tired, that's all."

As his father slowly moved off to the right, he spread his hands out to his sides, one hand still holding the cane. Ted knew what his father was doing and he, too, spread his hands out to make himself appear bigger to the cattle. He moved off to the left, moving just as slowly and quietly as his father. They would move around in a wide arc until they'd positioned themselves behind the herd. They didn't want to spook them anymore than they already were. They needed to push the herd to the west levee and back toward the front of the property. They needed to get the cattle to fresh water and feed. They would be okay after that. It would take some time, but like everything else, they would make it in the end.

{5}

Bayou Noir

It was Saturday afternoon and Luke LaCroix was riding in Dale Guidry's pickup. They'd knocked off work around noon and were now going fishing. With both windows rolled down, the loud roaring hum of the large gumbo mudders filled the cab.

"Where's this place again?" Luke shouted.

"Mais, how many times I gotta tell you?" Dale shouted back. "It's called Bayou Noir. So shut the fuck up about it, uh."

Now outside of town, Luke could smell the country air. They passed rice fields that had been recently harvested and the air was thick with the scent of rice chaff. It smelled like the part of the mill where the semis hauling raw rice into town were unloaded amid billowing clouds of rice dust. Luke glanced at Dale. The big man had a yellow welder's cap pulled down over his long frizzy hair. His beard tossed haphazardly in the open window, his face hardened and humorless. Dale wasn't acting like himself and it had Luke worried. For one thing, Luke had never ridden in the pickup when Dale wasn't smoking a joint. It's usually why they rode around in the truck at lunch, before returning to work with a good buzz on.

"Can you at least tell me where it is?" Luke said.

"Goddamnit!" Dale said. "It's on the way to fuckin' Intracoastal City, okay? What the hell do you care where it's at?"

"I was just wondering," Luke said.

Luke had come back home from college for the summer. His father had gotten him a job at the rice mill in town. Luke was put on the same maintenance crew that Dale worked on as a welder. In the beginning, Dale didn't like Luke. He nearly threw Luke off the roof one day because Luke had pissed him off about something. But after a while, Dale had softened and they became friends. Luke felt lucky that Dale had taken him under his wing. A big man like Dale was a good person to have as your friend in a place like the rice mill.

The day suddenly darkened as the pastures of cattle and rice fields gave way to an area called Grands Bois, a densely wooded swamp. Without braking, Dale pulled the truck onto the gravel shoulder. There was what looked like a dirt road that went into the woods and he turned onto it. The truck's big knobby tires skidded momentarily before biting into the loose gravel. Up ahead and crossing the road was an old barbed wire fence that had been neglected for some time. When the truck reached the fence line, Dale killed the engine.

Once off the highway, Luke could see that the road they'd turned onto abruptly ended after penetrating the swamp just beyond the barbed wire. As if the road had given up, conceding to the swamp. In the silence, Luke could hear the sounds coming from the forest, the high pitched droning of cicadas, the distant plaintive cawing of a crow, the deep, guttural moaning of bullfrogs near and far.

Luke couldn't see a canal or a bayou anywhere. There was only the sunken forest for as far as he could see. "Where the hell are we fishing?" he said.

Dale got out of the truck and gestured toward the swamp. "Mais, the fish are in there," he said. "Where you think?"

Luke didn't want to go into the swamp. Not for a stringer of sac au lait. He now understood why Dale had told him to bring hip boots. Luke was glad he'd brought his waders instead.

While putting on his waders, Luke slapped at his neck and his palm came away bloody. In the cool of the shade, and out of the direct heat of the early afternoon sun, the mosquitoes were active the way they normally were at dawn or dusk. He knew it would only worsen as they entered the swamp. He wished he'd known to wear long sleeves the way Dale had.

"Got any mosquito repelent?" Luke said.

"It don't do no good," Dale said. "Not in there."

Dale had his hip boots on and was now handing Luke a rod and reel. He seemed in a hurry to get started. "Make sure you line ain't loose," Dale said, "or you'll get it hung up like you can't believe."

They'd stopped to buy crickets at a bait shop on the way out of town. The crickets were now in two cylindrical bait cages, chirping on the floor of the truck. Luke put the string of one of the cages over his head so that it hung around his neck.

Dale took the other bait cage. Before shutting the door, he reached under the seat and pulled out a gun belt with what looked like a Colt 45 in the holster. A big, long barreled pistol. Dale buckled the belt around his waist. Then he said, "Let's go," and began moving toward the fence line, where the slack, rusty barbed wire hung low. With one hand on the fence post, Dale hauled himself over the top wire with the ease of someone half his size. Luke marveled at how effortlessly Dale managed his own great bulk—the way a bull, usually lethargic-looking, can in an instant overtake a man with the speed of a horse. Luke recalled the day on the roof of the mill earlier that summer, when Dale had chased him down before grabbing a fistful of Luke's shirt. He'd dragged Luke to the edge of the roof and threatened to throw him off. As if to make a point.

Dale was already moving toward the swamp and Luke carefully eased himself through the barbed wire. As Dale began walking into the water Luke hesitated. He didn't want to follow Dale into the swamp, but he knew he couldn't turn back now. He felt the waders grip his ankles as he stepped into the water. As though breaching some hidden boundary, the mosquitoes suddenly came alive. They were everywhere, swarming around his face, buzzing in his ears. He breathed in a mosquito through his nose and spit it out.

"Goddamn!" Luke said, slapping at the mosquitoes clouding around his face.

Without paying Luke any mind, Dale stopped and dipped his hand into the water. He appeared to be searching for something on the bottom. He came up with a handful of black mud, the sleeve of his thick khaki welder's shirt soaked from his elbow down. After removing the twigs and decomposing leaves, he rubbed the mud over the back of one hand and then the other. He smeared the mud onto his face and neck. The muddy water dripped from his beard and onto his shirt.

"What the hell are you doing?" Luke said.

"Trust me, you'll be glad you done it," Dale said.

His face now covered with the dark mud, the big man turned and began moving into the swamp. Luke quickly grabbed a handful of the swamp bottom before applying it to his exposed skin. It went on gritty and fetid, stinking of rotten vegetation and swamp gas.

With the mud covering his arms, face, and neck, Luke followed Dale again. He was still concerned with Dale's silence. He wished the big man would fire up a joint. Not because Luke wanted to get high, but because it would bring back the normalcy that was missing.

One day, not long after the incident on the roof, Dale had asked Luke if he wanted to smoke a joint. Right out of the blue. Luke didn't have any friends in the mill and was eating his lunch alone in one of the third story windows the way he'd done since the beginning of summer. After that, Luke was going with Dale to get high at lunch every day. They usually rode around town in Dale's pickup. Once, Dale had taken Luke home with him to his trailer and they ate lunch there. That's where Luke met Dale's wife, Yvette.

"How far is it?" Luke asked.

"A little ways," Dale said.

The bottom of the swamp was level and solid. Smooth walking, except for the occasional cyprus knee jutting into their path. The peat-stained water sat motionless and rose to about mid-thigh on Luke, just above the knees on Dale. The day grew darker under the thick canopy and was as cool as Luke had ever felt it in early August. Now the swarms of large biting flies had joined the mosquitoes in their dogged assault.

"How far we going?" Luke asked again.

Without turning, Dale said, "Mais, quit your fucking whinin', uh. Why you gotta be such a pussy about everything?"

They'd walked for what seemed like two miles, though it was hard to tell. Luke looked back from time to time, trying to keep his bearings. He'd lost sight of the truck almost immediately. Now he couldn't hear the traffic on the highway anymore.

Just then, the canopy parted as they came to a small clearing. Dale finally stopped. He didn't say anything as he began readying his rod and reel. Luke looked around and saw nothing that would indicate they'd arrived anywhere.

"Mais, c'mon, couillon," Dale said. "What you waitin' for?"

"Where we fishing?"

"You'll want to cast you line at that opening." Dale pointed at a spot on the water. "That's where Bayou Noir's at. You can see it if you look."

Then it became obvious as Luke could just make out a divide in the trees. He might have overlooked it had there not been a number of broken fishing lines snagged and hanging from the tree limbs across the channel, the red and white corks dangling like Christmas tree ornaments. Always the sign of a popular fishing hole, even in the middle of nowhere, even in the middle of a swamp.

They'd fished for about an hour in silence. They'd each caught ten or more fish. Mainly sac au lait and goggle-eye. Luke had caught a nice choupique and he could feel the big fish now tugging on the stringer that was tied to his belt and trailing behind him in the water. After reeling in another fish, Luke unhooked it. As he untied the stringer from his belt to add the new fish, he noticed the tail of a snake only a few feet from where he stood. It startled him, the way the sudden awareness of a snake always did. He dropped the fish he was holding and began moving away from the snake. As he moved, the snake moved with him.

"Shit," Luke said. He could see the tail of the snake still following, matching his speed.

"What's a matter?" Dale said.

"There's a snake after me," Luke said.

"Mais, he ain't after you," Dale said. "He's after you fish." Dale handed Luke his rod and reel. "Here, hold this."

Dale took the revolver from the holster. He cocked back its

hammer. Then he began lifting Luke's stringer slowly from the water. "Don't move," Dale said. As the last fish on the stringer came to the surface, a water moccasin could be seen with the tail-end of the fish in its white puffy mouth. The snake's jaw was unhinged, its broad triangular head already misshapen. It was trying to swallow the fish. Dale slowly held the stringer out at arm's length. He put the barrel of the pistol at the snake's head and fired, disintegrating the snake's head and the lower half of the fish. The sound of the gun was deafening and rolled through the swamp, echoing in the distance a long time. Like thunder on the horizon. Dale dropped the stringer back into the water, holstered the still-smoking pistol, and took his rod and reel from Luke.

"It ain't the snakes you gotta watch out for," Dale said, moving back to the spot where he'd been fishing. "It's the fucking alligators. Mais, they got 'em big out here, yeah."

"I was wondering why you brought that along," Luke said, referring to the pistol. Luke's ears were numb and ringing from the explosion.

Dale reeled in his line and recast it. "Mais, what you think I brought it out here for, uh?" he said.

"I don't know," Luke said. As the sun moved across the sky it filled the opening in the canopy above Luke and shone down on him blazing. It all at once felt like August in southwest Louisiana again.

"You think I brought it out here to shoot your skinny little ass, or what?" It sounded like Dale was joking, the way he said it. But it could've just as easily been taken seriously.

"I was hoping it wasn't for that," Luke said, trying to sound like he was going along with a joke.

"I wouldn't do it that way," Dale said, watching his cork bob on the water. When it didn't go under he jerked the line, teasing the fish below that seemed only interested in toying with the bait. Probably a little bream.

"Wouldn't do what that way?" Luke said, jerking his own line nervously. He didn't want to press the conversation, but he didn't think he should run away from it, either.

"Man, if I wanted to kill you, you think I'd be stupid enough to put a fuckin' bullet hole in you head?'

"So how would you do it then?" Luke said.

"Let's just say it would look like a accident," Dale said, hooking another sac au lait. He reeled it in, unhooked it and added it to his stringer.

"What's on your mind, Dale?" Luke said. "I mean you're really starting to freak me out, here."

Dale didn't say anything. He seemed to be contemplating something. Then he began to speak. "See that pole," he said, nodding his head at a bamboo pole sticking out of the water, the faint movement of the current against it. "It's a channel marker. Take one step past it and you'll go under like a rock. It don't look deep, but it's a lot deeper than you think."

It seemed like a strange thing to say. Luke watched Dale, waiting for him to continue, but he said nothing more. Luke had been using Dale as his mark, figuring that so long as he didn't walk beyond the big man's position he'd keep from walking into the bayou.

"I was gonna bring you out here and let you fall in," Dale said. "I was glad when I saw you'd brung you waders because it'd be a lot easier than with hip boots."

"Seriously, Dale. What the hell are you talking about?" Luke said. "I mean, why would you even say something like that?"

Dale was watching his cork as it moved in the slow current of the bayou that flowed silently beneath the surface of the swamp. "I couldn't hold you down," he said. "That'd be cold-blooded. That ain't how I am."

"Not cold-blooded?" Luke said. "How can you say that? Killing someone on purpose is cold-blooded."

"That ain't how I see it. There ain't nuttin' cold-blooded about a accident."

"But you're not talking about an accident," Luke said, "you're talking about murder. And any kind of murder is cold-blooded, Dale. It's why they call it cold-blooded murder in the first place. Ever think of that?" Luke realized he was sweating beneath the layer of dried mud on his face. With the sun pouring down on Luke, the mosquitoes and flies were now intent on Dale who stood off to the side, in the shade of a cyprus bough.

"Well, in my book it ain't murder if you just protectin' you own," Dale said, still fishing, still not looking at Luke. It was as if they were debating the different makes of pickup trucks or outboard motors and not the different degrees of murder. "You break into my house," Dale continued, "and I'd have no problem shootin' you ass. But to premeditate it, now that's somethin' else."

Luke couldn't understand Dale's logic. But the fact that they were talking about it led Luke to believe Dale had changed his mind and wasn't going to do anything after all. If Dale were going to do something, Luke knew, it would've already been over. Luke would be standing on the bottom of Bayou Noir, his waders filled with swamp water.

"So you're not planning on it anymore?" Luke said.

"Nah. I thought about it all the way out here, though. I was gonna do it, too."

"Why?"

"Because I could've swore you were foolin' around with Yvette, why you think?"

Yvette was a good deal younger than Dale, about Luke's age. Soon after the day Dale had taken Luke home with him for lunch, Dale was inviting Luke over all the time. Mostly after the late-night shift. They would clock-out at midnight before heading over to the trailer. Then Dale and Yvette and Luke would do bong-hits and drink a lot of beer. They'd watch TV and play bourré, sometimes late into the night. All laughing and having a good time.

"Do you really think I'd be crazy enough to mess around with your wife?" Luke said. "I mean think about it."

"It'd be a stupid thing to do," Dale said. "That's for damn sure. Especially for a fuckin' school boy."

Dale laughed and Luke laughed with him.

"Well, I know she's been messin' around with someone," Dale said. "For a little while, I was thinkin' it might've been you."

"What made you change your mind?" Luke said.

"I don't know. I guess it just didn't make no sense that you'd have the balls to follow me out here if it was you that was messin' around with her."

Luke didn't say anything. The black swamp mud on his face absorbed the heat of the direct sunlight. His face felt hot and the dried mud began to moisten with his sweat, reactivating the swamp stench. When Dale didn't say anything, Luke said, "Do you really think she's cheating on you?"

"I know she is," Dale said. "I don't know who with yet, but I'm gonna find out."

Again, Luke envisioned himself unwittingly walking into the sunken bayou. He saw himself struggling to stay afloat in the water-filled waders that would've pulled him to the bottom like cement blocks. The thought turned his stomach. He felt for a moment that he might vomit. He wanted to leave this place. He wanted to leave the swamp.

"I actually thought I could change her," Dale said. "I mean she swore she'd changed. She promised me she'd not be like that nomore if we got married." Dale had the butt of his rod stuffed into the front pockets of his jeans. He lit a cigarette and was now blowing the smoke at the mosquitoes and deer flies that shrouded his muddied face. The swarm quickly dispersed only to return just as quickly the moment the smoke cleared.

Luke didn't know what to say. He didn't know Yvette had been that way before. There's no way he could have known. But, now that he did know, he wasn't surprised. "I guess some people don't change," he said.

"Not people like her," Dale said. "God, what was I thinkin'? How could I've been so fuckin' stupid gettin' mixed up with a girl like her?" Dale reeled in his line and recast it toward the far edge of the channel.

Luke couldn't be sure, he couldn't see Dale's face behind the mud, but it sounded like he was crying. Luke looked away. He didn't want to see Dale like that. It sickened him to hear Dale sound so pained. To realize that a big man like him had it in him to feel that way. The more oblivious Dale was to what was actually going on, the more pathetic he seemed, and Luke wanted to be free of it. He wanted to leave this place. He wanted to ask Dale if they could go.

Luke thought about the nights out at Dale's trailer. He thought of one recent night in particular. It was after the night shift and Luke and Dale and Yvette were drinking and getting high. They were up all night playing cards and laughing and having a good time the way they had all those times before. Only on this night, Dale had passed out in his Lazy-Boy, leaving Luke alone with Yvette.

Luke continued to sweat and the mud was now wet again on his face and beginning to run. The foul odor had become as stong as when he'd first applied the mud back at the pickup. Luke positioned the rod and reel between his thighs. With his hands free, he attempted to refashion the wet mud on his face into a mask. He didn't want to be uncovered. He didn't want to be exposed to the swamp and to all that could harm him there.

{6}

Nostrils

"Look at the size of that thing!" Etienne shouted. "He's huge!"

Five men stood crowded onto the small pontoon platform that jutted out from the dock twenty yards offshore. Three of them stepped back from the edge as the alligator swam past. The shift in weight caused the platform to dip unsteadily. For a second, they all had to struggle to keep their balance. No one wanted to fall into the water.

Etienne said, "It's gotta be a fourteen-footer." He hadn't moved away from the edge, so he was able to get a good look at the creature. The alligator turned and made another pass. The platform sat several feet above the water, resting atop a collection of oil drums that had been lashed together with fat lengths of nautical rope. "Look at that," Etienne said, and he showed them the thick mat of black hair covering his large forearm. "My hair's standing on end."

Chris saw how the sight of the alligator amazed Etienne. He noticed the way it seemed to put a fright in the others. It wasn't just that Etienne was a Cajun. He'd hunted alligators with his uncle in the marshes of Louisiana. Everyone had heard the stories.

Wilson, Etienne, Chris, Allen, and Jason had been the first to arrive at the ten-bedroom lake house; the rest of the party would be coming that next day. There had been talk about the big gator that whole week and on the drive down from Dallas. They were told to not bother packing their swimsuits. No one would be getting into the water.

After the mad rush of claiming their bedrooms, they'd all run down the wooded hillside toward the boathouse. They hadn't stopped running until they'd reached the far end of the long, narrow walkway that connected the boathouse to the pontoon platform. They couldn't wait to see the alligator that was called Nostrils.

It was Wilson's parents' lake house. He'd brought along a small Styrofoam cooler with him onto the platform. In it was a fifteen-pound brisket. Wilson tied the meat to the end of a length of baling twine. Blood pooled on the platform's sunbaked planking as the twine bit into the slab of raw meat.

The alligator turned sharply in the water.

Wilson said, "Hold your horses, Nostrils." He tied the knot as quickly as he could. He seemed proud that the others were amazed by the big gator. He seemed especially satisfied that Etienne was so visibly impressed.

The other end of the twine was secured to a heavy bamboo pole. The alligator seemed to know the drill and continued circling, each time pausing in front of the platform.

"He looks almost playful," Chris said. As he said it, he wondered if that characteristic could be attributed to something as cold-blooded, tough-skinned, and knobby as an alligator. Chris watched Etienne leaning on the lamppost at the corner of the platform, all his weight hanging out over the water as he took in the spectacle of the alligator. He appeared more excited than afraid, and Chris realized, maybe for the first time, that Etienne wasn't tall. That his barrel-chested stature somehow made him appear taller than he actually was. His darker skin and the ability he had to grow a beard in a day seemed to give him an authority that no one dared question when it came to things pertaining to the outdoors.

The pole bowed as Wilson swung the heavy brisket out over the water. The gator seemed reluctant and Wilson raised and dropped the meat several times so that it splashed the surface of the lake. Then they could hear the alligator taking in a long, deep breath of air through its enormous nostrils before disappearing, hardly swirling the water.

"Where'd he go?" Jason asked, sounding disappointed. He craned his neck so he could see the water without having to step any closer to the edge of the platform. "I think you scared him away."

"He hasn't gone anywhere," Etienne said in a way that reminded everyone he knew about these kinds of things.

"Look, there he is. See the air bubbles?" Wilson said, pointing at the water.

They all watched as a trail of what looked like champagne bubbles rose from the depths, showing the alligator's position beneath the water as it moved toward the meat. Then they could make out its rows of jagged white teeth as it ascended, mouth open. It broke the surface, slowly took the meat in its jaws, then again disappeared below the surface of the water. The pole bowed deeply for a moment until the rope snapped. Then the alligator was off and cruising away from the platform with the brisket in its mouth. It reminded Chris of a submarine the way it pushed a swell of water above its nose. Everybody cheered, still standing back from the edge of the platform.

As if curious about something, Allen took a tentative step closer to the edge. He peered down at the water where the gator had just been. To give him a scare, Jason quickly moved in and gave him a shove, holding his T-shirt so he wouldn't fall into the water.

"You asshole!" Allen shouted, springing back, his face knotted in terror.

Everyone else laughed nervously, and the group took a step away from the water. No one wanted to fall victim to the same prank.

"Man, don't even clown around like that," Allen said. "That's all we need is for someone to get mauled by an alligator. Fucking trip would be over before we even tapped the keg." Allen laughed, but the color had drained from his face. He looked anything but amused.

"Maul, hell. He'd swallow you whole," Jason put in, like he'd seen it happen a hundred times.

Everyone nodded in agreement.

"You'd be surprised," Etienne said, still hanging on the lamppost. "They're actually shy. Believe me, it's more afraid of you than you are of it."

"That's such bullshit," Jason said.

"I'm serious," Etienne said.

Jason looked at Wilson. He said, "Tell Etienne he's full of shit."

Wilson said, "I know I wouldn't jump in the water."

Etienne said, "I'm telling you, we could all go swimming right now and it wouldn't do anything. It might not leave entirely, but it'd keep its distance. I guarantee, it's more curious than anything else."

Jason shook his head. His voice took on a tone of condescension. "I'm not saying you don't know about alligators, but I'm calling bullshit."

For a reason no one understood, Jason had always had a problem with Etienne. Maybe it was because Etienne had a weird first name. Or an even weirder last name that no one could pronounce. Maybe it was because Etienne wasn't a part of the main circle of friends. Etienne was a geologist, and not in advertising like everyone else, and that seemed to alienate him as much as anything. He only came around because he was Allen's friend. In fact, any time Allen had parties at his house, Etienne would invariably be there, cooking a big pot of gumbo or sauce picante or something else spicy that made everyone sweat. This was Allen's bachelor party, so it was only natural that Etienne be there, too. He was in the wedding party like everyone else who would be at the lake house that weekend.

Jason stabbed a finger toward Etienne. "C'mon, admit it. You're full of shit, aren't you?"

Jason was a good deal taller than Etienne. Still he would never have talked to him like that had Etienne not been so good-natured about everything. Chris realized he wanted Etienne to punch Jason in the mouth.

"Tell you what, Etienne," Jason said. "If you really believe Nostrils is so harmless, then jump in."

"Shut the hell up, Jason!" Allen had finally come to his friend's rescue. "You don't know him. He'll fucking do it."

And he did do it.

Without taking off his shoes or his shirt, Etienne handed his beer to Chris and jumped in. Everyone was screaming. Chris braced himself as they rushed toward the edge of the platform, making the deck tilt forward dangerously. There was an instant when Chris thought everyone was going in. When Etienne surfaced, Wilson already had one end of the bamboo pole in the water next to him.

"C'mon, Etienne, grab the pole!" Wilson shouted. "Hurry!"

Etienne now faced the alligator. Already finished with the large brisket, Nostrils was no more than twenty feet away.

Etienne calmly waded in the water, hardly making a ripple, staring down the alligator.

Chris looked at the others, at the awe in their faces. No one was screaming anymore. They were quiet, watching to see what would happen next. Then Chris had the sudden urge to jump into the water with Etienne. If they hadn't expected Etienne to jump in, they'd sure as hell never expect him to. Chris took a step toward the edge of the platform and realized he wasn't afraid. He looked out at Etienne, at his broad back rising out of the water. There was something animalistic in the way he hovered there. He didn't seem out of place the way he should have, swimming with an alligator. Chris knew he'd be safe in the water with him. Etienne knew about these kinds of things. But before Chris could jump in, Wilson pushed him aside, keeping the bamboo pole within Etienne's reach.

Jason was all at once screaming hysterically, sounding strangely like he might start crying. "Okay, you proved your point! Now get the hell out of there, you goddamn freak!"

That's when the alligator slowly dipped beneath the surface of the water, leaving a slight swirl and then a single eddy where its large head had been.

Everyone was screaming again. Chris laughed; not because he thought it was funny, but in place of anything else he could think to do to express the way he felt about what was happening.

"Damn it, Etienne, don't be an idiot!" Wilson was shouting again. "Grab the fucking pole!"

Etienne slowly turned in the water and casually breaststroked toward the platform's rusty ladder. Before making it halfway up the ladder, he was being pulled onto the deck by anyone who could grab hold of him. He fell awkwardly onto his face on the warped boards of the platform deck.

"Unbelievable," Chris said. His hand was shaking as he handed Etienne his can of beer. "Man, why did I have to leave my camera up in the room?"

"What the hell did you do that for?" Wilson was still shouting. He looked like he might punch Etienne. He wasn't happy.

Allen said, "Man, if you're going to commit suicide, at least do it on the day we're leaving and not when we just get here."

Etienne said, "I'm telling you, I wasn't ever in any real danger. See, it isn't even around anymore." He took a long drink from the beer. Chris wondered if anyone else noticed how Etienne's hand was shaking.

"Unbelievable," Chris said again, thinking to tell Etienne how he'd thought about jumping into the lake with him. How he almost did.

Etienne took another thirsty gulp from his beer, then burped. He looked at Chris with what appeared to be a triumphant smile.

———

That night Etienne and Wilson sat on the back deck overlooking a hillside dense with trees, and the lake beyond that. Rib-eyes hissed and sizzled on the large, stainless steel grill. The sliding door was open so that the music from the stereo inside poured out into the night, drowning out the night sounds that were nothing like in the city. The other men were inside playing poker. Etienne and Wilson drank beer from the keg while keeping an eye on the steaks. On the upper rack of the grill, away from the flames, Etienne had placed whole mallard ducks, strips of venison, and slabs of redfish fillets.

"I should've brought some alligator meat," Etienne said. "Some back-strap or a tail roast. That would've been appropriate, huh?"

Wilson smiled.

"And they'd never know what they were eating until we told them," Etienne said. "Imagine the looks on their faces."

They both laughed. Then they were sipping their beers without talking.

After a moment, Wilson spoke, as if he'd been looking for the right moment and this moment was as good as any. "Admit it, you were scared out there in the water today."

"Are you kidding? Talk about I was scared."

"Then why the hell did you do it?"

"I don't know."

Etienne remembered jumping into the lake. He remembered facing the big alligator, his vision level with the surface of the water, so staring straight into the alligator's eyes. It dawned on him then that the name Nostrils was fitting.

"I guess I just wanted to put Jason in his place," Etienne said. "Does he ever shut up?"

"Man, you can't let him get to you." Wilson stood at the barbecue pit, prodding the two-inch thick steaks with a long-handled fork. The meat spit fat into the flames that leapt hungrily at the grease.

Wilson put down the fork. He returned to the chair next to Etienne and dropped into it heavily. He said, "You let someone like Jason get the best of you and the next thing you know you're jumping into a lake with a fourteen-foot alligator."

They both laughed.

And then they were quiet again.

Etienne listened to the chorus of night sounds, or what he could hear of them over the music. He wondered if any of them had ever sat in the wilderness and just listened to the night.

"I'm just glad there weren't any other gators around," Etienne said, knowing the dynamic is different when there's more than one in the water. "It would have been a different story, that's for damn sure. You know, competition and all that."

"I know. I've seen it before."

"What do you mean?" Etienne said, thinking Nostrils was all the experience Wilson had ever had with alligators.

"I mean I've seen it happen before. Right out there."

"There used to be other gators out here?"

"Used to be? They're still here."

"You're kidding?"

"No."

"Well, why the hell didn't you tell me?" Etienne sat up in the chair and looked at Wilson.

Wilson chuckled. "You never asked. It never came up. Hell, how was I supposed to know you were gonna go and jump in the lake?"

"I didn't see any others around."

"I'm sure they're there now. They know they'll be fed whenever there's anyone here. It's a big lake so it sometimes takes a while before they make their way over."

Etienne wasn't listening to Wilson anymore. He fell back into his chair and was now thinking of what might have happened. His mind was back in Louisiana, in the marsh at Rockefeller Refuge. Hunting and trapping weren't allowed within the confines of the vast refuge, so the alligators there had a chance to grow big without the chance of being killed for their hides.

Within the refuge, there were many weirs that regulated the water flowing into and out of the marsh. One such weir that Etienne and his father frequented was a gathering place of sorts. Whole families might be there, crabbing on the bank or from the walkway atop the weir itself. Men threw cast nets, hauling in baitfish and shrimp. Others with rods and reels cast their lines from flat-bottomed boats anchored just shy of the weir, where the water spilling from the marsh into the canal attracted redfish, drum, speckled trout, and flounder. And there were always a number of big alligators there. Some as big as ten or twelve feet, waiting for a handout. The gators had grown accustomed to it and were continuously jockeying for position around the boats, always anticipating something hitting the water.

One day, a boy in one of the boats had snagged his hook on a small branch along the bank. He was with his father and their Labrador Retriever. The boy reeled his line in taut and then pulled on it until the branch he'd hooked into broke away from the bush. After reeling in the small branch, the boy unhooked it and, without thinking, threw the branch back out into the water. The boy's father seemed to know what had been set into motion even before the branch hit the water. The dog jumped from the boat and was swimming toward the branch, instinctively going out to retrieve it. The three biggest alligators were on the Lab before anyone could do anything. And then it was gone, never making a sound as it went under. The water churned in the distance as the three gators resurfaced. The yellow dog appeared limp, already dead, as the gators, still in a tug-of-war, began twisting violently. They tore the dog apart.

The man was crying. He scolded the boy, who still didn't seem to understand what had happened. It was quiet around the weir as the man pulled in the boat's anchor, started the motor, and then left, the whole time crying. It was something Etienne would never forget.

"Goddamn," Etienne said, his mind now back on the deck with Wilson in East Texas. He felt numb.

"And you're right about the competition thing," Wilson

said. "Nostrils is a different animal when the others are around. There's nothing shy about him then. He wouldn't have hesitated the way he did today."

"Shit," Etienne said. "They as big as Nostrils?"

"No," Wilson said. "But I'd say they're still pretty big, though."

Etienne didn't say anything. The incident at the weir was playing itself out again in his mind.

———

Chris said, "All I'm saying is that I think it was the most incredible thing I've ever seen." He rearranged the cards in his hand. Then he threw a chip to the center of the round table.

"It was fucking crazy," Allen said.

"No, it was fucking stupid." Jason added a chip to the pile. "Think about it. Who the hell jumps into the water with an animal that's big enough to swallow you whole? I mean, goddamn!"

Everyone laughed and shook their heads.

Allen said, "Did you see the way he stared it down? I thought he was going to wrestle it or something."

"Ain't dat what they do for fun down dare on duh bayou?" Chris said, using his best Cajun accent, sounding more like he was from Brooklyn.

"It was stupid," Jason said again. "That's all it was. Etienne's nothing more than a swarthy coon-ass fishing for attention. So you should all just stop talking about it."

Jason glanced at the open door that led out onto the deck where Etienne and Wilson were tending the range. Seeming certain that he couldn't be heard over the music, he continued. "You saw how he ate it up. I mean, c'mon, he was so fucking pleased with himself."

"Man, what's your problem with him, anyway?" Allen said. "All I know is you dared him to do it and he did it."

"And all I know is it wasn't that big a deal," Jason shot back. "If it were a crocodile—now that'd be a different story. But it wasn't. It was an alligator. A fat, lethargic alligator that had a chunk of meat the size of my thigh still stuck in its throat."

Allen said, "That's such bullshit. Just admit it. You dared him to do something you never thought he'd do in a million years, and he did it. That should've shut you up, so why are you still talking?"

"I'm telling you, that gator is so fat it couldn't catch Chris. And he swims like a girl." Jason smiled because he knew Chris was giving him a look.

"Well, there's only one way you're going to prove that," Chris said. Again, he thought to bring up how he'd almost jumped into the water with Etienne. How he was about to before Wilson stopped him.

"I agree," Allen said to Jason. "Either you jump in tomorrow, or shut the hell up about it. I'm tired of your shit. I think we all are."

"Okay, you'll see," Jason mumbled. "Tomorrow morning."

———

Mid-morning the next day, Jason, Chris, and Allen were out on the pontoon platform. It had been a late night, and they were all hung over, if not still a little drunk. It was already hot out on the lake, and Allen had his shirt off, exposing his pasty belly. He sat in a lawn chair with his head thrown back and his eyes closed. Chris had a camera and was taking pictures, while Jason lazed about the deck, silent with his headache, drinking a beer.

The platform vibrated with someone coming down the

long walkway. It was Etienne, looking fresh from a shower. His black hair still wet, the shadow of a beard beginning to show, dark and full.

"Morning, y'all," he said.

Everyone said Etienne's name.

Etienne saw that someone had brought out an ice chest. He reached in and grabbed a beer from the still-cold water, the melted ice from the night before.

"Hair of the dog," Etienne said. "I can't seem to get enough of it."

"Man, you aren't kidding," Allen mumbled without opening his eyes. He sounded sick.

"There's two more alligators," Chris said, looking back at Etienne. Chris sat Indian-style at the edge of the platform. He wasn't hanging his legs over the side the way he might have had there not been three big alligators in the water. "See, there's three of them now."

There were three alligators just off shore, all big, each over eight feet in length. Still, they were a good deal smaller than Nostrils. Etienne looked out at the lake. The sunlight on the water made it difficult to see anything. Then he saw the big gator just to the right of a small islet, maybe two hundred yards offshore. It appeared monstrous even at that distance.

"These are different," Etienne said. "There's Nostrils out there. See?"

They looked where Etienne pointed.

Chris' camera had a long zoom lens attached to it. He pointed the lens at the gator and focused. He said, "Yep. That's him, all right."

"Why doesn't he come over?" Allen asked, looking up and shielding his eyes from the glare.

"I can't believe he'd be scared of these three," Chris said. "Think it's because he's outnumbered?"

"No, Nostrils has the run of the lake," Etienne said. "Don't ever think different."

No one said anything. Even Jason seemed to take Etienne at his word.

"Wilson's about to come down with some more meat," Etienne said. "Nostrils will be here fast enough once the meat starts hitting the water. I guarantee it."

Etienne realized he'd grown attached to the big alligator. He was talking about it as if it were a pet dog and not some freakishly big reptile.

Etienne decided to run up to the house for his own camera. He wanted to be back before Wilson came down with the meat. "I'll be right back," Etienne said. He put down his can of beer on the deck. Then he was off, running down the narrow walkway toward the boathouse, his weight, for a moment, violently shaking the platform and everyone on it.

"Is it me," Jason said, "or was it peaceful out here before he showed up?"

"God, there you go again," Allen said.

As the platform shook, Chris noticed that Jason had taken an exaggerated step away from the water.

The long bamboo pole with the twine tied to it lay on the platform deck where Wilson had left it the day before. Jason picked it up and began striking the water with it. It appeared to frighten the three smaller gators and they quickly dipped beneath the surface, all at once. Suddenly, and almost imperceptibly, Nostrils began making his way toward the platform, so slowly that the water around him remained calm.

"It's working," Chris said, still watching Nostrils through the zoom lens. "Here he comes."

Seeing Nostrils coming toward them, Jason began striking the water harder and more rapidly.

The three other gators had resurfaced. As Nostrils increased his speed, a small wake began to emerge.

"I want a copy, okay," Allen said to Chris, who was snapping off another picture.

Chris checked to see how much film he had left in the camera. He said, "Well, Jason, here's your chance to prove you're a man."

Jason said, "Okay. How much will you give me if I go in right now?"

It seemed to catch Allen by surprise. He sat up in his chair, his bloodshot eyes mere slits. He said, "Hundred bucks."

"Two hundred," Jason countered.

Chris said, "What are you talking about? Etienne did it for nothing. Hell, I would've paid you ten-thousand bucks yesterday before he went in and proved that nothing will happen."

"Two hundred," Jason insisted.

"Okay, I'll pitch in a hundred," Chris said, certain Jason would never do it.

Jason hesitated. "Before I do anything," he said, "I want the money in my hand."

Chris said, "You mean it isn't enough to be immortalized in a picture?" He was looking through the lens, not imagining Jason in the picture, but himself and Etienne, both staring down the big alligator. Thinking back to the day before, Chris realized that he'd really not been afraid to jump in. He wasn't afraid now, the way he could tell Jason was.

After grabbing his camera from the bedroom, Etienne

hurried down the large, sprawling staircase. He stopped in the kitchen where Wilson was running hot water into a sink filled with large chunks of red meat.

"I forgot to take it out of the deep freezer last night," Wilson explained. He stood next to the sink with a beer in one hand, a cigarette in the other.

"What does it matter?" Etienne said, moving toward the refrigerator. So long as he was in the kitchen, he figured, why not grab another beer?

"Ever try to tie frozen meat with a rope?" Wilson said and Etienne understood what he meant. "It won't take long," Wilson added. "It just needs to thaw out a little."

"Got a drill?" Etienne said. "Bet if we tied the rope through a hole in the meat, it'd take 'em forever to work it loose. Especially if it was frozen."

Just then, the sliding door slid open and someone ran across the living room toward the bedrooms at the back of the house. It was Allen. "Hey, you've gotta get down there. Jason's gonna do it."

Etienne and Wilson looked at each other for an explanation. After a moment, Allen came running from the back of the house and was in the kitchen with Wilson and Etienne. He was winded and gasping for air; as much, apparently, from the run up the hill as from the excitement of whatever was going on at the lake. He held what looked like a handful of cash.

Allen said, "C'mon, you don't want to miss this."

"What's going on?" Wilson said.

Allen was beginning to regain his breath. He said, "It's so obvious he's backed himself into a corner. Now he has to do it. There's no way he can back out." Before going on, Allen held up the money so Jason and Etienne could see it. "Not when I give him this. C'mon!" Then he was off, running toward the door.

"What the hell's he yammering about?" Wilson said.

"I don't know, but I think we'd better get down there."

Outside on the deck, they could see that Allen had stopped midway down the hillside. He'd met up with Jason, who was coming from the direction of the boathouse. After hurrying down the hill with Wilson, Etienne could see that Jason looked sick. He had vomit down the front of his T-shirt. Then Allen was off and running again, out of the woods and toward the boathouse. He was screaming something in a way that gave Etienne a bad feeling.

Wilson said, "Jason, What happened? You get sick?" Wilson made the face someone makes when smelling vomit.

"Chris!" Jason said.

"What about him?" Wilson said.

Etienne and Wilson quickly stepped back as Jason vomited in the leaves and pine needles at their feet.

"I swear, I didn't think he'd do it," Jason said, now dry heaving. He was crying. "I swear. I never thought he'd do it."

Now Etienne felt sick as he ran toward the lake, the incident at the weir slowly playing itself out again in his mind.

{7}

Christmas Eve

Nick and Anna spent the better part of the morning in each other's arms, speaking very little that whole time. They lay on the futon in the livingroom, naked beneath the sheets and sweating even though it was freezing outside and everything remained under a thin crust of hardening snow and ice. When the fire in the fireplace died down, Nick didn't add another log. Anna didn't ask him to. The large picture window overlooking the street was fogged over.

She would have to leave soon. Her husband was at home loading up the car. She knew he would have the twins dressed and ready to go by now. She was supposedly out doing some last minute shopping and he could call at any minute. She avoided looking in the direction of the coffee table where her cell phone sat silent, like a bomb ready to go off at any second and there was nothing she could do to get away from it.

Now she lay on her side, facing away from Nick. As if no longer hot and unwilling to be touched, he rolled over and snuggled up against her back, his body shaping hers. When he kissed her on the neck, she trembled and began to cry.

"I don't want to go," she said again. She'd been saying it all morning. And, like all the other times, Nick didn't say anything in return. But then, what could he say? He wasn't married and, as much as he referred to the problem as their problem, it was in reality more her problem and they both knew it.

"At least you don't have to deal with your family," she said, because Nick had decided to stay in Dallas for the holidays. "At least you don't have to pretend to be happily married."

It was true. She dreaded it now, having to go through the motions of being a wife to a man whom she didn't exactly dislike, but wasn't in love with anymore, either. Ironically, she'd been sleeping with her husband more frequently than she had in some time, because she didn't want him to suspect anything. And that wasn't easy. The way her husband eagerly accepted the change, as though thinking there was a sudden rekindling of their relationship, had struck her as pathetic. Now even the idea of making love to him—or allowing him to make love to her—began to repulse her in a way she could no longer bear. She'd never been able to sleep with men she wasn't in love with. She'd never slept around in high school or college or any other time in her life. A part of her wished she had, or at least had the capacity to do so without it bothering her.

Now she was about to go on a road trip that could take as long as ten hours because of the deteriorating weather conditions. She planned on sitting in the back seat with the twins, playing games. She didn't want to have to talk to her husband. She would have to pretend to be sleeping. Or she would have to act like she was reading the book she'd been carrying around a lot lately for that purpose.

"I wish you were going home," she said, still facing the fireplace. She noticed that the logs, while no longer ablaze, still glowed red, giving off a great deal of heat, as if gutting it out one last time before growing cold and dying out altogether.

"Why should it matter if I go home or not?" Nick said.

"I don't know. I just hate the idea of you being here all alone for Christmas. It's sad."

"I'll be fine," he said, nestling his nose into the cleave at the nape of her neck as he spoke. "Besides, I'd be just as lonely and miserable at home with my family as I'd be here by myself. At least here I won't have to act like I'm having a good time."

"See, that's not fair," she said, not crying anymore. "In the meantime, I'll be in Amarillo with my whole family watching me, looking for signs. I know my parents can tell something's wrong. I can hide it from the man I'm married to and live with, but I can't hide it from my parents on the phone. Isn't that the most ridiculous thing? I know my mom can't wait to get me alone so she can start digging." She sighed heavily, feeling like she might start crying again. "God, I don't want to go," she said.

Nick didn't say anything. He pulled her closer to him on the futon and she could feel him beginning to harden again against her.

She wished she were going home with Nick, and not her husband. Then she might have the kind of Christmas she used to have. Not so long ago, she'd thought Christmas was the most romantic time of the year and not the most depressing. She realized she was waiting for Nick to ask her to stay, although she wouldn't have—couldn't have—even though she wanted to. She realized she needed something to get her through the holidays, something to hold on to, even if only hopeless assurances. But he didn't say anything.

{8}

Brother

"Goddamnit, Robie, what the hell you gawkin' at?" John Dubois said without taking his eyes off the road. The cigarette clamped loosely between his lips jumped as he spoke, sending the dead ash onto the front of his camouflaged hunting shirt.

"I'm not gawkin' at anything," Rob said. He turned and looked at the darkness outside his window.

It was four a.m., the day after their father's funeral, and Rob was with his brother heading toward Pecan Island. All the musky odors of a dog clung to the inside of the pickup, masked only by the cigarette smoke that hung in a low lying cloud at the ceiling of the cab. John had been smoking non-stop since they left Abbeville. Rob glanced at his brother again in the darkness of the cab, the only light on his face the yellow glow from the dashboard. Rob searched for something familiar. He tried to remember the last time he'd seen his brother. It'd been twelve years earlier, he knew that. That's when his brother had suddenly left Abbeville for good. At the time, Rob had been twelve years old. Suddenly, it dawned on Rob that he had known his brother for as many years as he didn't.

John had smoked for as long as Rob had known him. It had become a part of his physical make-up, the way a mustache had for their father. If John had been smoking two days earlier when he entered the house, Rob might have recognized him sooner. Rob remembered how he'd scored his first cigarettes from John. At the time, his brother had said, "gotta start sometime," before handing Rob what was left of the pack he had in his pocket. That was probably twelve years ago, Rob realized, maybe one of the last times he'd seen him. Rob didn't smoke anymore, but, sitting in the smoke-filled cab now, he wanted a cigarette. "Mind if I bum one of those," Rob asked.

And just as all those years earlier, there was no hesitation. As John shifted his hands on the wheel, he reached into his shirt pocket and pulled out a cigarette before handing it to Rob.

The few memories of them together that did stick out in Rob's mind, besides the cigarette incident, were of them hunting with their father. So when his brother asked him the day before if he wanted to go hunting Rob had jumped at the opportunity. At the time, Rob thought it a good idea, a way to get to know John again. They could talk. There's little else to do in a blind in the middle of a marsh. But now that they were on their way to Pecan Island, Rob wished their father were there with them. He had been a buffer between John and Rob, a buffer that was noticeably missing in the truck now.

It was bitterly cold outside, near freezing. At first Rob wanted to back out of the hunt. He didn't want to leave the warmth of his bed. Rob didn't like hunting in the cold or the rain the way most duck hunters did, the way you were supposed to if you were a duck hunter. He was like his father, who might go, but reluctantly. His father would be bundled up and bitching the whole time he was out there freezing in the blind—until he could stand it no more and went home. With his limit of ducks or not, it didn't matter. Often having to leave John to find his own way back to Abbeville, because he refused to leave the marsh. Contrary to Rob and their father, John preferred hunting in that kind of weather. The colder, the wetter, the better. Nothing could keep his brother out of the marsh during hunting season and Rob knew they would be out there all day if it took that long to limit out.

In Forked Island, they stopped at Jack's, a dilapidated old convenience store that stood as the last outpost before the road crossed over the Intracoastal Canal. At that point, the road was raised above the flat wetland, a wide canal paralleling on either side, and then the marsh that went forever in both directions. Their father had always stopped at the old store so they could get something to eat and refill their coffee mugs.

John and Rob left the warmth of the truck and were now outside in the cold. Rob couldn't help dreading what it would be like in the marsh, where it always felt ten degrees colder in the absence of any windbreak. At least it was overcast, he thought. If it were clear, there might be ice on the water. He took one last pull from his cigarette before flicking it at the gravel parking lot. He felt the dampness in the air and hoped it wouldn't rain.

Rob rounded the bed of the truck. He checked on John's dog to see how it was doing. The Chesapeake Bay Retriever looked like a brawler. It had a scarred face, and was husky for a female. Still, when Rob had walked out of the house that morning, he found the dog curled up on the doormat, trembling uncontrollably. Rob tried convincing John to let the dog ride inside the truck with them. The odor in the cab indicated that it had before, and often. But John insisted on making the dog ride in back, as though wanting to prove how tough it was. Rob studied the dog now, and it seemed fine. It was busy gnawing on a decoy. Rob could see it was a mallard drake decoy and the dog had been chewing on it a good while, mauling its green head.

"No!" Rob shouted at the dog. "Shit, John, look what your dog's doing." Rob wanted to slap the dog in the head, but hesitated. It wasn't his dog. Instead, he forcefully pushed the dog away from the sack of decoys, at the same time realizing it as a stupid move. He didn't know this dog well enough to assume it wouldn't bite. But the dog didn't bite him. The decoy held no importance, the way a bone or a bowl Dog Chow might.

"Goddamn you, Lady!" John shouted, suddenly taking on a deeper, more menacing voice. The dog retreated to the corner of the bed and away from John. John circled around the truck until he was back over the dog. He took the mangled decoy and began beating the dog savagely over the head with it. "See what you did?" John shouted at the dog, holding its collar. He showed the dog the chewed up decoy before continuing with the beating. Other hunters in their rolled down hip boots and camouflage were walking up to or out of the store. They watched, unmoved, as if seeing someone doing a necessary thing. Something they'd all done with their own dogs at one time or another for ruining a perfectly good mallard decoy.

John and Rob left the dog trembling in the bed of the truck. They entered the store where a number of men sat circled around a space heater talking French. "Como ça vas?" John said.

One of the men said, "Bien, bien. Et tu, bébé?"

Rob wondered if his brother spoke French, if he'd managed to pick it up from their grandparents the way Rob hadn't been able to.

For as long as Rob could remember, there was free coffee at Jack's. Rob moved to the pot and refilled his mug. He bought three links of hot boudin, which he would eat in the truck. Then he thought to buy two bags of venison jerky in case they did stay out in the marsh beyond lunch. From what Rob could see, his brother bought a two-day hunting license, two six-packs of beer, a honey bun, and a loaf of bread. Once outside the store, John tore open the bread and tossed it unceremoniously into the bed of the truck. Seeming to have forgotten the beating it had just received, the dog set upon the loaf like it hadn't eaten in a week. "Good girl," John said.

John put the beer in the same ice chest that had been sitting outside the back door of the house since he arrived two days earlier. He'd been drinking from it ever since, as if it held an endless supply of beer. There was still beer in it now, and ice and water. John added the two six-packs to the chest.

Rob could tell his family thought it strange that John would keep his beer in the ice chest and not in the refrigerator inside the house. But it was John and no one said anything, like it was just another example of what they had come to call his eccentricity. As if that made it easier to explain the things he did that they didn't understand. If his father had been around, it would've led to a fight. And that would have led John to storm out, leaving for a couple of days or a week before returning as if nothing had occurred. It was always the same. Then, one time when John stormed out, pissed off about something inconsequential, something no one seemed to remember, he didn't return. Months later, he sent word that he was in Idaho, working on a ranch, like it had been a plan that everyone knew about.

The ice chest was now in the bed of the pickup, along with the heavy 16-horse Go-Devil. So that the long-shafted outboard motor would fit, they had to angle it diagonally in the cramped short bed of John's truck. Rob assumed John had bought the beer for after the hunt. But then John took a couple of beers from the chest. "You sticking with that?" he said, referring to Rob's mug of coffee.

"Yeah, I'm good for now," Rob said. "Maybe after the hunt."

"Suit yourself." John got back behind the wheel and twisted off the cap of one of the beers. He took a long thirsty gulp before putting the bottle between his thighs with the other bottle.

Rob never drank before or during a hunt. His father had taught him that. Even men at the hunting camps, who were generally drunk most of the time, at least waited until after a hunt to resume drinking. Rob was glad his father wasn't there, knowing this would have led to another altercation.

John had insisted on driving. Just as he'd insisted they hunt with his dog and not Rob's. Seeing the mess John's dog was making, Rob was now glad they weren't in his truck. The dog still hadn't taken a shit yet. It was only a matter of time.

The back window of the cab slid open and shut, giving access to the bed. Without slowing on the dark, narrow two-lane road, John had reached back several times, letting in the frigid air. With one arm through the window, he opened the chest for more beer, while, at the same time, fighting off the dog that desperately wanted into the warmth of the cab. On one occasion, when the window was open, Rob tossed the skins from his boudin into the bed. The dog inhaled them without chewing. By the time they arrived in Pecan Island, some twenty miles later, the first six-pack was nearly finished.

It was five o'clock when they reached the private landing. They parked the truck with the headlights on, facing the water, so they could see as they loaded and readied the boat. Through the mass of swarming insects that had been drawn to the light, they could see the mud boat and two flats. The mud boat sat in the water, its bow and stern lines tied to stakes driven into the soft bank. It sat docked beneath a makeshift boat shed—corrugated tin atop four slender creosote posts. The two flats were out of the water and resting belly-up on the levee. There was little time to work. Sunrise was less than an hour away. Rob quickly went about the business of hooking up the Go-Devil to the transom of the twelve-foot flat.

"Why aren't we using the mud boat?" John said, sitting on the tailgate, lighting a cigarette.

"We can use it if you want, but even if we get it started here, there's no guarantee it'll start again when we're ready to come back."

Rob thought to tell John about the time earlier that season when the mud boat broke down on them at the end of a hunt. His father and the other two hunters weren't in any shape to walk in a marsh, let alone out of one. It'd taken Rob two hours to reach the landing. He'd never trusted the mud boat after that.

"Where we hunting?" John asked. Rob knew he meant where, as in where on the property. John knew this marsh as well as anyone. He just didn't know where the blinds were. They moved them every year or two, keeping it fresh. Rob had been flattered that his brother wanted him along. Only now did he realize that John needed him there. He would never have found the blinds without him.

"I figured we'd hunt toward back," Rob said.

"Why not the hotel?"

The hotel was what they called their father's blind. It was large and could accommodate four hunters. As hunting blinds go, it was comfortable.

"It's all hunted out. The ducks are in back now."

Rob had already loaded into the boat his and John's shotguns in their carrying cases, a metallic ammo box, the push pole, and the sack of decoys; even the ice chest, which sloshed with the remaining bottles of beer and icy water. Rob worked with his gloves off. He didn't want to get them wet. His hands, soaked now, had grown numb. He felt a cutting pain as he pulled the rope the several times it took to crank the motor started. Then he locked the motor in an upright position so it could warm in the morning's bitter cold.

John's dog was out of the truck. It had pissed on the three boats and the taller of the surrounding ant piles. Now it was off running in the distance, its near-black coat making it invisible in the darkness. It barked at something, probably one of the Brahma cows that grazed in the pasture that ran to the canal fronting the marsh. Rob hoped the dog would take a shit before getting into the boat.

John still sat on the tailgate. He struggled to get his large feet into a pair of waders. He'd not taken the boots with him to Idaho, so hadn't worn them in twelve years. He had one boot on and was winded. He looked drunk.

"Damn it! I think my feet got fatter."

John finished another beer while catching his breath, a cigarette between his lips.

"You about ready?" Rob asked.

Rob assessed his brother. He seemed more like a stranger all the time. Rob could see the contrariness that always drove his father so insane with anger.

"Goddamn boots!" John said, tossing the empty beer bottle into the darkness.

———

Finally underway, Rob stood at the back of the boat. In one hand, he held the long shaft steady in the water as they motored down the dark, narrow ditch. In his other hand he held a large Q-beam flashlight. He directed the beam over his brother's head and at the water in their path. Since it was overcast there was no moonlight. John sat at the front of the boat, weighing down the bow as it plowed through the water. He had his hands in his pockets, a beer between his legs, and a cigarette centered in his chattering teeth. He had his back to the wind, so was facing Rob. The dog occupied the middle of the flat. John shouted at it to sit still, but the dog ignored him, moving from side to side, slipping and skidding on the wet, muddy aluminum floor, barking excitedly at the darkness on either side of the boat. Rob kept a wide stance, fighting against the dog's shifting weight.

They left the ditch and entered a wide, deep canal. In the narrow, pronounced beam of the flashlight, Rob scanned the water for anything that might be in their path. It was too cold for alligators, but there might be debris; a log, a tree, a dead cow. Rob was keenly aware of his brother's condition and the fact that he was wearing waders. If the boat flipped here, John's waders would quickly fill with water and he'd sink to the bottom. It happened sometimes. People died.

Moments later, Rob was relieved to be out of the canal. Now they headed down another shallow ditch, this one no wider than the boat. The ditch ran the length of the marsh that was their property. As they entered the first of a series of small lakes, Rob pointed the flashlight at their father's blind as they passed it, illuminating the many decoys on the big pond.

John looked and nodded. "The hotel," he shouted, and Rob smiled.

They continued on toward the back blind. If the hunting was slow there, Rob figured, they could then move to the grass on the edge of a small pond where he sometimes saw flights of mallards. That had been his plan, anyway. It's why he'd brought the sack of decoys. But now, seeing John drunk, Rob hoped the blind would do. He didn't want to have to deal with a man in John's condition in the marsh grass that rooted itself in the soft, deep mud. He imagined his brother bogged up to his waist, stuck until Rob could work him out.

Suddenly, John was shouting something. He said, "I think we should hunt dad's blind."

"I told you, it's all hunted out."

"I still think we should hunt it. For dad."

Rob understood what he meant. It was strange, though, hearing it come from John. Rob thought they'd only come out to hunt. He'd missed the point.

"Alright," Rob said. After some effort, he managed to turn the boat around before heading back toward their father's blind.

Finally there, Rob was happy. He'd unloaded everything and now stood in the blind. There was no other place he'd rather be than in the marsh before dawn. The sound of the breeze as it blew through the roseau reed camouflaging the blind. The sounds of poul d'eux and nutria coming from near and far. It was the time he enjoyed being with his father most. When they would stand there in anticipation of the hunt. Sometimes talking, sometimes not, but enjoying a common thing. He wished he were with his father now and not this drunk man. He'd never really known John, so he didn't seem like a brother at all, or what he thought a brother was supposed to seem like. Still, Rob was glad John had made the suggestion to hunt in their father's big blind. The hotel.

John had already uncased his gun. He had taken several beers from the chest and put them on one of the empty seats next to him. It was quiet enough to hear the foghorns coming from the oil platforms in the gulf. Rob heard the sudden high-pitched whine of a mosquito. If his father were there, he would have already lighted a cigar to keep the mosquitoes at bay. In his father's absence, and in wanting to at least have some part of his father there, Rob pulled a cigar from his shirt pocket. He'd taken two from his father's cigar box at home. He'd planned on saving the second cigar for later. Instead, he handed it to John.

"It'll keep the mosquitoes away better than that," Rob said, gesturing toward the cigarette John was smoking. John flicked what was left of the cigarette into the pond. It hissed as it hit the water. The dog, standing in the mud outside the blind, thought to pounce on it.

"Antonio Cleopatra!" John said, recognizing his father's brand. John lit both cigars with his Zippo. He was clearly excited and Rob was glad he'd given him the cigar.

"So where do you live again?" Rob said.

"Idaho," his brother said. "You already know that."

"I know," Rob said.

The smell of the cigar smoke reminded Rob of his father, the way cigar smoke always did.

"I wish dad were here," John said, and Rob wondered if the smoke were working on him, too.

"Yeah, me too," Rob said.

Just then a flight of teal flew over. In the suddenness of it, they both ducked. Then they could see the fast moving birds, their rapid wing strokes in the dim light of the eastern sky where the sun still hung below the horizon. Where the gray sky blushed rosier all the time. The teal fanned out before regrouping and continuing on and out of sight. John had already brought his gun up and had it leveled off at the ducks.

"Shit," John said. He seemed embarrassed that he'd reacted the way he did. "You never get used to that."

Rob felt the adrenaline surging through him that John was talking about. Rob decided to uncase his gun and load it. It was almost time. Then John loaded his gun and Rob realized that his reaction to the teal had been just that: a reaction, without intention.

"They got any big ducks come through here, or is it still all teal?" John asked.

"It's still the same, I guess. A lot of teal early, then the mallards and pintail come in later."

"I wanna get four greenheads," John announced.

In the distance, they could hear a mud boat racing through the marsh. It sounded like a truck speeding down a lonely country road. The sound came downwind so it seemed much closer than it actually was. A beam could be seen several miles away as someone in the boat lighted the way. The motor slowed, idled, then shut off as the boat reached its destination. They could hear voices, a dog barking. John's dog whined.

"They're getting out a little late," John said.

Rob agreed. He hated getting out late. But he didn't say that. Instead he said: "Why didn't you come back when dad was sick?" It had been eating at Rob for some time. His mother had anguished over it the whole time their father was in the hospital, the outcome certain.

John didn't say anything.

"I mean, you knew he was sick." Rob finally felt it was okay to talk about it with this man who was his brother. "Mom said she told you. She said she told you he wasn't going to make it."

John remained quiet, puffing on his cigar. He scanned the sky, seeming indifferent.

Rob kept talking. He said, "They were sick about it, wondering if you'd come home or not."

John chuckled. "Robie."

"What?"

"You don't get it do you?"

"What?"

"They weren't afraid I wouldn't show. They were afraid I would."

"You can't really think that."

"No, I don't think it. I know it, because it's true."

Rob knew he never understood the relationship John and his parents had. Rob had been a kid the whole time John still lived with them. Rob had to remind himself that his parents didn't hold John in the same light that Rob did. While John's move to Idaho may have seemed romantic to Rob, it was considered strange to his parents. Eccentric.

"Did he ask about me?" John said.

Rob said, "He wondered where you were, if that's what you mean." In truth, Rob didn't remember his father ever asking about John. It's as if he assumed John would never show up and so didn't expect it. He didn't put the energy toward something he knew would never happen. He was a lot like John in that way.

"No, I mean did he ever ask for me?"

"He wasn't really talking a whole lot," Rob said, which was true. After Rob had gotten everything off his chest, as if he'd only been given a moment to do so before his father died, there was nothing left to talk about. Then when his father didn't die right away they were left with all that time and nothing else to say. After that, when Rob had taken his turn in the chair next to his father's hospital bed, little was said. He'd sit there for hours at a time, never saying a word. But then, being there seemed to be enough for the both of them. They each seemed to draw comfort in that. Thinking of that now, Rob realized that his brother would have only disturbed that peace. He would've shaken things up, as his father might have said, at a time when things didn't need shaking up.

It was light now, and Rob watched the sun break the surface of the marsh, a large red ball that looked like another star altogether and not the sun.

The dog still stood up to its elbows in the thick mud. Rob could hear the suction-sound made from the dog pulling its legs up and out of the mud before setting them back down again. The dog wasn't used to the marsh. It had better realize, Rob was thinking, that there was no staying above the mud. Otherwise, it would tire out before the hunt even started.

Just then, John rose from his seat and fired twice. Rob turned in time to see two ducks, wings folded and falling to the pond. The dog was on its way before the birds hit the water.

"Damn, I didn't even see 'em coming," Rob said, thinking that John was as good a shot as he ever was. If his father were there he would've beamed with pride. He always enjoyed watching John shoot, a spitting image of himself. The only thing they had in common, it seemed. It was a bond that Rob could never share in, no matter how much he tried. His shots were never as clean, as instinctual.

"I would've warned you, but they were on us before I could say anything." John slid two purple shells into the chamber of his Model 12 16-gauge pump. It was the same kind of gun their father hunted with.

The dog brought back one duck before retrieving the other. Two gray ducks that Rob mistook as mallards in the still dim lighting.

With the two ducks in the blind, Rob and John now stood motionless. After a while, Rob was reminded how cold it was. His ears ached and his nose was raw and running. His toes numb, he stomped his feet on the plywood floor.

"Goddamn, it's cold, uh," John said, not looking to Rob like he was cold.

"Man, you aren't kidding," Rob said. "I just hope this breeze holds up. If it doesn't, you can bet it'll rain. Watch."

"C'mon, Robie. A little rain never hurt anyone."

John scanned the sky for ducks. He reached into his coat pocket and brought out a pint of scotch. He cracked the paper seal and then took a short swig from the bottle.

"Here," John said. "This'll chase away the cold." He handed the bottle to Rob. "I meant to dig up dad's hunting flask before we left, but I guess this'll do."

Rob took the bottle from John. He thought back to the first time he'd ever drunk scotch from his father's flask. He was still too young to have his own blind, so was hunting with his father in The Hotel. His father had offered the flask to Mr. Theriot first, a man who'd hunted with them often back then. After Mr. Theriot had taken his turn, Rob's father handed the flask to Rob. Like it was no big deal.

"To dad," Rob said. He tipped the bottle back and let the scotch pour down his throat. It warmed his chest and belly as it went down. He took another long sip before handing the bottle back to John.

"To dad," John said. He held the bottle out toward the pond, as if toasting the decoys. Then he hit it again, only this time putting away half the bottle. John made a face like he'd gulped down rancid milk. "I wish they'd had dad's label at that store," he said. "Anything but this rot gut shit." He handed the bottle back to Rob.

"It's funny," Rob said. "Dad was so against drinking in the blind and now here we are drinking to him while standing in his blind." Rob sipped from the bottle. He handed it back to John.

John continued to scan the sky. "Well, I came home for three reasons—drinking and hunting being two of them. Figure I won't be here long, so here's to killing two birds with one stone." John took a sip from the bottle before chasing it with a big gulp of beer.

Rob didn't know what John meant, so didn't say anything. There wasn't anything to say. He looked around the blind, realizing it was now fully light out. Dawn had crept up the way it always seemed to. Rob noticed the spent shotgun shell casings in and around the blind. Most were purple, from the "Sweet Sixteen" his father hunted with, like the one John was hunting with now. And the cigar butts and wrappers, all left by his father.

"It's what dad would've done if he could've," John said, and his tone seemed to change.

Rob wasn't sure what John was talking about. He wondered if John might cry.

"You didn't know that," John said, "but it was dad's dream to move west. You think he wanted to live in Abbeville the rest of his life?"

"So why didn't he?"

John chuckled. "Because of me, that's why."

"Why, what did you do?"

"I was born, that's what I did." John laughed. "I'm why he married mom." He wiped at his eyes with the back of his glove.

"Where'd you ever get that idea?"

"You didn't know dad very well, did you?"

Rob took offense. "I sure as hell knew him better than you ever did."

John smiled.

"What?"

"Robie," John said.

"Stop calling me that. I'm not a kid anymore."

"Okay, Rob," John said. "I guess there's still a part of me that sees you as a skinny twelve-year-old."

"Well I still say I knew dad better than you think I did.

Hell, what do you know, you weren't even here for the last twelve years."

"Look, Rob. I was your age when I left, so let's just say we both knew him equally, okay."

John was right, Rob thought. Rob didn't know why he felt it necessary to argue about it. They sat quiet, scanning the sky. They could see flights of ducks off in the distance. They watched to see which way they would turn.

"If you knew him, though," John said, "you'd know that his dream was to move away from here. He had big plans. Then when mom got pregnant granddad gave them the piece of property where the house is now. That's why we grew up here. You didn't know any of that, did you?"

Rob felt he was hearing about a family that wasn't his own.

"By the time you were born," John continued, "he was already deep in the rut. He wasn't going anywhere and he knew it. Hell, he made the best of the situation, I'll give him that much. He did good. So there isn't any reason you should've known. But I could always tell he resented me because of it. And he never let me forget it."

Rob didn't doubt there was a conflict between John and their father. He'd seen it often enough. There wasn't any reason not to believe it.

Rob said, "He really enjoyed the pictures you sent home." Rob thought of the smile on his father's face as he looked at the pictures and postcards John sent home from time to time. A lot of what Rob knew about John came from these pictures. Often showing his brother looking rough and unkempt and in the company of other rough and unkempt men. Posing with an elk he'd shot. A bear. A stringer of pheasant. Pictures meant for his father. The picture Rob favored and had framed sat on the dresser in his bedroom. It showed John on horseback, a herd of cattle in the background, snow-topped mountains beyond that.

"He never admitted it," Rob added, "but I could always tell he was excited to get them. He kept them, you know?"

"I figured he'd appreciate it," John said.

"I thought you were sending them home to rub it in his face or something."

"That's the last thing I wanted to do. I wanted to show him that we'd made it. Maybe he couldn't live his dream, so I was for him."

Rob said, "I wish he would've told me all this."

"It's not like he ever told me either. I just figured it out, you know. I pieced it together until it finally made sense."

"So then why didn't you ever tell him all this?"

"I couldn't. I mean I wanted to. I almost did come home when he was in the hospital. But he would've resented me for it. I know it sounds weird, but I think it was enough for him to see that I was doing it. If I'd told him why I was doing it, then he would've thought I was rubbing it in his face. That make sense?"

"I guess," Rob said, but he wasn't sure. It was too much to think about all at once. "He thought you were shacking up with an Indian squaw," Rob thought to add.

John chuckled, not saying anything; neither admission nor denial perceptible in his smile. The clouds sagged lower in the sky now and Rob was sure it was going to rain. Just then John began calling and Rob froze in his seat. He didn't want to give up their position to the ducks. He looked at John so he would know where the ducks were. John stopped calling, still watching the ducks circling until his eyes showed they had moved behind them.

"Got three mallards coming around," John whispered. Rob could hear John click off his safety. Rob clicked off the safety of his gun and waited. "They looked interested. They'll probably be coming from your right. You take the hen and I'll go for the greenheads."

They both sat motionless, waiting. They could hear one of the ducks calling from behind. It sounded right on top of them. Rob could see John smiling, as they heard the whistling of their wings overhead. Then, there they were, just as John predicted. Three mallards coming in, feet down. They looked heavy as they dropped belly first toward the outer edge of the pond.

"Now," John shouted, and they both stood and shot. The ducks tried reversing themselves, but it was too late. The hen and one of the greenheads dropped to the water. "Nice shot!" John said.

Rob had fired twice, but was sure he'd shot behind the hen both times. They were farther out than he'd thought. He was surprised to see it drop. "I didn't think I hit it," Rob said, his heart racing. He cracked his 12-gauge over-and-under and ejected the two spent and smoking shell casings. He inserted two new shells into the barrels. His hands were shaking.

"The wind does funny things," John said, reloading his gun. "But you plugged her good, I'll give you that."

Rob kept replaying the moment in his mind. John wouldn't have let the other greenhead get away had Rob taken care of the hen. He was certain of that. It's what his father used to do, Rob thought now, what Rob called charity kills. When younger, Rob wasn't a very good shot. It frustrated him that he couldn't hit the ducks as easily as his father and brother. His father knew this and would sometimes shoot the ducks at which he knew Rob was shooting. Then he'd claim Rob had hit them. Rob looked at John and, seeing that he wasn't making a big deal about it, decided to let it go. He'd accept the charity, choosing, instead, to be flattered by it.

The breeze had died and now in the damp stillness it began to drizzle. Rob pulled the hood of his hunting jacket over his head and hunkered down for a long day in the marsh. Even with the two mallards and two grays already in the blind, there was a lot more shooting to do before they limited out.

John looked up at the sky and regarded it with a smile. He stuck out his tongue to catch the rain. "Man, it's gonna piss on us all day, isn't it?" John said. The idea seemed to amuse him.

"Looks like it," Rob said, not seeing any breaks in the clouds. His cigar already soggy, he tossed it outside the blind. It landed amid his father's many cigar butts, scattered in the whip grass and mud.

They were quiet again and Rob listened to the sound of the rain pelting the waterproof fabric of his hood.

"Would you mind if we got out of this?" John said.

"You want to leave?"

"I think we did what we came out here to do. There's no sense in over doing it. Besides, I don't know why anyone would want to sit in a blind all day in the cold rain just to kill some poor little ducks."

Rob smiled. It sounded like something his father would've said, like something he would've said to John.

{9}

Big Damn Pears

Luke LaCroix first told Old Green about the pear tree one day at lunch. They were outside off the boiler room, sitting in the shade of the overhang. The day was hot—it was early August in south Louisiana—but it was hotter in the rice mill where the air was thick, stagnant and reeking of diesel fumes. When Luke had pulled the large pineapple pear from his paper sack, he noticed the old man's expression suddenly change.

"Ever see a pear this big, Green?" Luke said as he unfolded his pocket knife. He began carving away a large bite-sized chunk from the heavy fruit, the juice dripping onto the legs of his jeans.

"Mais, that's a big damn pear, yeah," the old black man said, pausing over his pot of rice and gravy. Every morning when he got to work, Green would place the old, pocked and dented cast iron pot on top of the boiler where the pot's contents, usually rice and gravy and some cut of meat, would keep warm until lunch hour. Green appeared to contemplate the fruit with covetous eyes. "Boy, where you get that at?" he said.

"There's a tree full of them in my parents' back yard," Luke said. Green was typically an emotionless, taciturn man. Luke had been working with him that whole summer and had never seen him intrigued by anything before. "Want me to bring you some tomorrow?"

Green cracked a thin smile at that, showing the few worndown, yellowed teeth he still had remaining in his mouth. "It's true?" he said. "You can bring me a couple?"

"Tell you what," Luke said. "Follow me home after work and you can pick all you want. Like I said, my parents have a whole tree of 'em that they'll never get around to picking."

However slight it was, Green's smile vanished as quickly as it had appeared. "I don't know," he said, returning his attention to the rice and gravy. He pulled a small lamb shank from the pot and inserted the meaty end into his mouth. After working the shank around his mouth for a moment, the bone came away clean and greasy.

"C'mon, Green," Luke said. "You can pick as much as you want."

"Mais, no boy, I can't do that," Green said. "It ain't my place."

"What are you talking about?" Luke said. "You'd be doing us a favor."

Green didn't say anything and Luke knew from his experience with the old man that he'd dropped the subject. There was no use talking about it anymore.

———

Luke had finished his junior year in high school in May. His father was good friends with the big boss over at the rice mill in town. As a favor to Luke's father, the big boss had agreed to give Luke a summer job. On his first morning at the mill, Luke met the big boss in his air conditioned office. After filling out a lot of paperwork, Luke followed him into the mill where they met up with a shift foreman. Luke stood there as the two men mumbled something in French to one another that Luke couldn't hear. Then, without saying anything to Luke, the big boss turned and walked away. The shift foreman then began moving toward the back of the the mill, and Luke followed him.

They passed through several cavernous rooms, each rumbling with machinery the size of automobiles that shook the old, worn plank flooring beneath Luke's feet. Deep into the mill and beyond the noise, they entered a dimly lit room, the only sound coming from a motor high in the rafters that labored to crank a chain that turned the workings of a grain elevator. Toward the rear of the room, Luke could just make out the back of a short black man as he worked alone, shoveling a pile of rice back into the conveyor from which the rice had spilled. In the half-light the man appeared as if a shadow. He had his shirt off and his back muscles could be seen rolling thickly beneath his taut, purple-black skin, glistening wet. As they approached him, Luke realized the man was old, but had the physique of a much younger man. Luke figured he must have shoveled a lot of rice in his life to look like that. The foreman introduced Luke to the man, saying his name was Green, but that everyone in the mill called him Old Green. The foreman told the old man that Luke would be working with him that summer. He said little else before turning and walking back toward the front of the mill. Luke was nervous being left alone with the old black man. As nervous as the old man looked to be left alone with Luke.

As Luke pulled into the long driveway of his parents' house, he checked his rearview mirror. He no longer saw Green following him and he wondered if the old man had changed his mind again. Then, as Luke pulled into the carport, he could see Green's pickup slowly turning the corner. It seemed to approach the house tentatively.

"You get lost?" Luke joked when Green had finally made it down the driveway. The old truck sat in the carport, its engine running loudly, a strange ticking sound coming from under the hood.

The old man didn't say anything. He slowly scanned the acre of property, the manacured lawn, the several moss-draped century oaks. He studied the large two-story house and then the kennel in the sideyard where the two yellow labs were going crazy. Luke shouted at the dogs to shut up, but they only continued barking, jumping hysterically on the wire enclosure. Luke shouted at them again and they settled down, but reluctantly.

Green looked terrified, as if certain the dogs would break through the kennel gate, padlock and all.

"Sorry about that," Luke said. "I don't know what's gotten into them. I guess they're not used to strangers."

Green didn't look like he wanted to get out of the pickup, he didn't look like he would. He said, "Boy, you sure you momma and you poppa say they don't mind?"

"Nah, they're not even home yet," Luke said. "C'mon, the tree's right around in back."

Green killed the motor, and the old truck went quiet. The door screeched open on its rusty hinges as he got out of the pickup. He appeared deliberate in his movement, as if walking on ice. As if trying to walk as silently as he could in his big, filthy work boots. The old man followed Luke toward the pear tree that sat amid a citrus orchard in the back yard, just up the hill from the bayou.

"You catch you some fish in there?" Green said, gesturing toward the bayou.

"Yeah. But I've sat there and caught plenty of nothing before, too, I can tell you that."

"Mais, me, if I lived on a bayou, I'd be fishin' all the time, yeah."

"Hell, Green, I didn't know you liked to fish," Luke said.

"I like catchin' fish," Green said, showing his few teeth for an instant, "but I like eatin' 'em more."

"Well, if you like catfish, this is the place to catch 'em," Luke said. "At least when the garfish and choupique aren't fouling up your line. They got a lot of that, too."

"I like catfish," Green said. "I like garfish and choupique, too." The old man was still studying the bayou, where the lush, just-mown lawn met the bank. He appeared to be looking at a shady spot beneath a willow tree where Luke usually sat when he fished in the bayou. On hot days, it was the coolest spot down there.

"I'll tell you what, Green," Luke said, "you can fish here anytime you want. How 'bout that?"

"Mais, I don't know."

"Seriously," Luke said. "I can tell you want to. Besides, you wouldn't be hurting anything."

Green looked away from the bayou. He turned his attention to the pear tree, as if changing the subject.

"Go ahead and start picking what you want," Luke said. "I'll go inside and grab something to put 'em in." Luke moved quickly toward the back door. Before entering the house, he added, "I mean it, Green. Pick all you want."

Old Green didn't say much to Luke the first week they

worked together. Luke would show up in the morning, clock in, and then grab the grain shovel out of his locker. Then he'd begin searching for the old man, the whole time feeling the cold, menacing stares of the other men as he moved deeper into the mill. Once Luke found Green, he would join the old man, blending into the labor of shoveling rice. They would go hours without saying a word. Luke marveled at the old man's steady, dogged pace.

Each day that had passed that first week, Luke felt more alone in the mill than he did the day before. The other men didn't want him there. They resented him as much as they seemed to resent Old Green. They would leer at the both of them as they took their breaks at the coffee pot with the rest of the men. Luke knew why they disliked him: he was a rich, white school boy that didn't belong in the mill. But he wondered what they had against Old Green.

One morning, Luke and Green were on the roof shoveling rice at a fast pace, trying to get the job done before the day's heat set in. Luke could tell the old man had begun to warm up to him a little. They'd been working together almost two weeks. Green still wasn't talking to Luke, but Luke felt he could now talk to the old man if he wanted.

Without stopping in his work, Luke said, "Why don't the other men like you, anyway?"

The old man continued shoveling, not breaking stride, and Luke didn't think he was going to answer. Then he said, "Boy, it ain't me they don't like. It's you. And now you with me."

"What do you mean," Luke said.

"What do I mean, uh? Boy, you know the big boss. And he put you in here with us. Now nobody is gonna have nuttin' to do with you."

"Or you," Luke said, now understanding.

"That's some kind a shit, uh?"

Luke didn't say anything.

"Summer will be gone soon," the old man said. "And then you'll be gone, too."

Luke felt awful for putting Old Green in that position. Still, he was all Luke had in the mill and he continued to follow the old man to the coffee pot for breaks and to the boiler room for lunch. Luke could tell the old man didn't like it, but he never said anything either. He'd accepted Luke as if having to. Like a blister on his toe that he could do little about but wait for it to go away.

———

Luke wasn't in the house long. He went to the kitchen and grabbed a grocery sack from the pantry. Before going back outside to the orchard, he took a look in the fridge to see what there was to eat. He was always hungry after a day at the rice mill, like he couldn't get something into his stomach fast enough. He ate a chicken leg as quickly as he could and then moved toward the back door. Through the window, he could see that his father was now home; his pickup was parked in the carport. When Luke looked toward the orchard, he saw his father talking to Green. The old man appeared small in the presence of Luke's father, standing there staring at the ground, his shoulders slumped, the small pile of pears that he'd picked on the ground at his feet. He had the demeanor of someone being chewed-out by a shift foreman.

Luke went outside. His father now home, the dogs in the kennel were barking again. They were jumping on the wire and going at it as savagely as before. Luke shouted at them to shut up, but this time they didn't listen to him and continued with the racket. Luke moved quickly to the orchard. He could tell his father wasn't happy about something. He

was talking in a tone that Luke recognized. Luke had heard it
before when in trouble, usually the times before his father let
him have it with a belt.

Luke's father turned and saw Luke approaching. "This
man says you told him he could pick pears," he said. "Is that
true?"

"Yeah, this is Old Green," Luke said. "He's the man I work
with at the mill. I told him to follow me home."

Luke's father seemed to unstiffen. He was still mad, but
now for a different reason. Maybe because he was put on the
spot and made to feel embarrassed, Luke wasn't sure. Luke's
father turned back to Green. "I hope you'll accept my apol-
ogy," he said. "I didn't know."

Green kept his eyes on the ground, not saying anything.

Luke's father turned to Luke. "You can give him what he's
already picked," he said. "Then he'll have to leave."

"I told him he can have all he wants," Luke said, showing
his father the sack he'd retrieved from the house. "We were
gonna fill this up."

"You heard me," Luke's father said. "It isn't open for discus-
sion. We can talk about it later."

"I just don't see how we're doing anything wrong," Luke
said.

"I said drop it," Luke's father said. "I mean it."

"But why?" Luke said.

"Okay, you want to talk about it?" Luke's father said. "Then
let's talk about it. You brought him here to my house, that's
what you did wrong." Then Luke's father turned to Old
Green. He said, "You know what I'm talking about, don't
you? I bet you understand."

Green's eyes remained on the ground. He appeared para-
lyzed and it was quiet as Luke's father waited for the old man
to acknowledge the question. Luke could hear the dogs in

the kennel still going at it, still barking. He could tell Green wanted to leave, that he didn't want to be there.

Luke looked toward the bayou, trying to understand. He looked at the shady spot beneath the willow tree and understood that the old man wouldn't be fishing in the bayou behind the house after all.

Without saying anything more, Luke's father turned and walked toward the house. He opened the back door and went inside.

"I'm sorry, Green," Luke said. "I don't know what got into him. I swear, he's not like that."

Green didn't say anything. He began moving toward his truck, as if finally able to move again. He left behind the pears he'd picked, still in a small pile on the ground.

Luke gathered the pears and put them in the bag as quickly as he could. He wanted to pick more, he wanted to fill the bag. Instead, he ran after Green who was already getting into the old pickup.

"Here, Green," Luke said. "At least take these." Luke reached through the passenger side window and put the bag of pears on the seat.

Green started the truck. He didn't look at Luke.

"I'll see you tomorrow, Green," Luke said. "First thing in the morning, I'll come find you, okay?"

The old man still wasn't looking at Luke. He still wasn't saying anything. The dogs in the kennel were going at it and Luke shouted at them to shut up. But they wouldn't stop.

{10}

A Return to Glencoe

He pushed his daughter on the swing, counting out loud with each push. He hadn't reached twenty yet when she told him to stop. He didn't want to; in the past, he'd always given her a hundred pushes. But she sounded irritated and, feeling the sting of a reprimand, he backed off. Then she was pumping her legs and he realized she was able to swing herself now, unlike the last time he'd taken her to Glencoe Park, almost two years earlier. When the perfect world he'd created for he and his daughter had come to a complete and sudden end.

He stepped to the side and watched her swing, her face beaming with little-girl exertion, her ponytail wagging wildly, her red, bare hands gripping tightly to the chains. He pulled a cigarette from his shirt pocket and lit it. The air was cold and damp, bitter, and he wished he'd thought to grab a jacket in his rush out of the clinic. He hoped it wouldn't rain. Or, worse, sleet.

It was then that the woman and her little girl arrived. He heard the car coasting up the street, pebbles popping under the tires, and at first he thought it was the police cruiser that had slowly driven by twice already. The woman parked at the curb, got out, and opened the backdoor. Then they approached the play area, which was set in an enormous sand box, all surrounded by a raised concrete-curb perimeter. Until that moment, the woman had been leading the girl by the hand. But now that they were at the edge of the play area it was the little girl who was leading her mother; tugging on her hand, hurrying her toward the swings where he was smoking and watching his daughter. It reminded him of the way his own daughter used to take off in a rush at the sight of another kid having fun, on the slide or the monkey bars or swinging on a swing. As if wanting to share in the fun she saw, as if wanting to steal it away and make it her own.

The woman wore white furry earmuffs, pulled down and clamped to a full head of curly blonde hair. She was short and heavy, but probably not as heavy as she looked in her pink puffed-out ski parka. The little girl wore a similar pink jacket, only hers showed an ample sprinkling of tiny cartoon bunny rabbits. She had her mother's hair. He could see several inches of it protruding from the base of her red and green Christmas-themed stocking cap, topped with a pom-pom the size of a baseball.

The woman looked at him, as if sizing him up, like she wasn't sure what to make of him in his purple medical scrubs. She appeared to be staring at the ID badge he had clipped to his shirt pocket. Seeing him with his daughter seemed to put the woman at ease, though, as if a man with a little girl couldn't possibly be threatening. She nodded hello.

"How's it going," he said, all at once conscious of the cigarette. It suddenly felt out of place at the playground and he searched for a way to get rid of it. Maybe that was the reason for the woman's disapproving look. He didn't know that either, but it made sense. He wasn't finished with the cigarette—he'd taken only four drags, with six remaining. He pulled on it hard, hoping to make up the difference. Then, when the woman wasn't looking, he forced himself to drop the still-smoking cigarette. He buried it in the sand with the toe of his tennis shoe.

The swings were set high, intended for older kids, and the woman had to lift her daughter onto the thick rubber seat that bowed to shape the little girl's narrow bottom. He remembered having to do the same thing with his own daughter when she was that age. A few years earlier. And just as his daughter had done, the little girl squealed with delight as the woman began pushing her. Not too high, but high enough for a little kid. With each push, making loud animated whooshing sounds that startled the little girl and had her giggling with fright. He smiled at the sound of the laughter and his eyes grew wet as he felt something turning inside his chest.

The woman's nose was already red and running, like she'd been outside longer than the two or three minutes she and her daughter had been at the park. Her heart clearly wasn't in it, she looked miserable. "You warm enough, honey?" the woman asked her daughter, not sounding like she wanted to be at the park on a winter's day. For an instant he wondered if his daughter was cold—he could see her breath, he could see his own—but then just as quickly decided she was fine. She was dressed for the cold. Besides, they had been to the park in worse weather than this. Many times. For the first five years of Julia's life, he was a stay-at-home dad. His wife was a lawyer and worked long hours. She traveled a lot. So it was just he and his daughter most of the time.

The woman's daughter continued to squeal blissfully, not appearing ready to go anywhere. He chuckled and, again, the woman gave him a hard look. Maybe she didn't think he looked like a typical father, he didn't know. He knew he didn't feel like a typical father. Not any more. He was still getting to know his daughter again and felt vaguely like a stranger. Like an imposter. But that was more because of the way she was acting. She still wasn't talking to him. She treated him like a friend of the family or an uncle or a teacher, and not a father. Apprehensive. Polite and not clingy the way she'd once been, the way he remembered. He hoped he hadn't lost her. He still wasn't sure if he had.

The woman's cell phone rang inside her coat pocket and she stopped pushing her daughter. Hardly a second passed before the little girl was screaming for her mother to keep pushing her. "Just a sec, sweetie, let me see who it is," the woman said. She glimpsed the screen of her phone before flipping it open and answering it. The little girl kicked her legs wildly, wanting to swing as high as his daughter, he knew, because it's the way his daughter was when that age. A real fire-eater. Invincible. Incapable of visualizing herself falling off the swing and severely injuring herself the way she so easily could have. The way she did that one time.

The woman had turned her back to him and he couldn't hear what she was saying into the phone. He wondered what she was saying.

He said, "Remember when you were a little girl like her, Jules?" He still couldn't believe his daughter was almost seven. It was hard to believe she was that old. "I brought you here every day. Without fail," he said, hoping to refresh her memory, trying again to initiate conversation. He just wished she would talk. "We'd dig in the sand and make sand cakes. I pushed you on the baby swings over there," he said, pointing to the miniature swing set for toddlers, situated alongside two miniature, plastic slides—one straight and yellow, the other blue and curvy. "Then when you got bigger, about this little girl's age, I started pushing you on these swings here. It was like a milestone in your life the way you acted. You were so proud, you know. Feeling like you were finally a big kid swinging on the big kid swings."

He remembered instances like that clearly enough. He remembered the things they used to do together and the fun they had. That wasn't the problem. What he couldn't seem to remember was himself and his daughter—especially his daughter—in the pictures. Like faces blurred in a photograph. And that troubled him, because he'd sworn he would never forget. He'd sworn she would never forget either. He had taken steps to ensure they would both remember. It's how it had all started, why he'd begun making their times together both as fun and routine as possible. After a time, it had become essential, in fact. Because by making it routine, by keeping it precise, he'd reasoned, they would both remember. It had all been part of a larger plan. As if he'd been preparing for all that would happen, even though he couldn't possibly have known at the time what was going to happen.

They'd started riding the trolley downtown every day, always after returning home from the park and Julia's afternoon nap. He would allow her to wear anything she wanted and she would invariably choose from one of the princess gowns on the rack in her closet—usually pink, always frilly. They would catch the 4:35 at West Village. Always eating Oreos— three cookies apiece—as the trolley rumbled squealing and squeaking through uptown and then downtown; his daughter on the edge of her seat, an indelible smile across her face, the plastic tiara in the tangle of her hair and off-kilter. Winning the hearts of everyone they came across in her absurdly adorable costumes. Always sitting in the front on the same bench. The trolley drivers had quickly grown accustomed to seeing them, they saw them every day. They began letting his daughter pull the cord that sounded the trolley's air-horn until that, too, became part of the routine.

Once downtown, they would go to the Dallas Museum of

Art and he would walk her around on his shoulders, looking at all the paintings, her warm, damp little fingers tugging at his hair the whole time. Next, they would walk to Cathedral de Guadalupe. They would time it so they'd get there at six o'clock, on the hour and in time to hear the ringing of the Angelus. Then they would watch the forty-nine-bell carillon that was exposed and could be seen from the street. The bells swinging wildly, all situated and stacked according to size in racks within the towering spire. After that they went home, still with plenty of time to have supper ready before his wife got home. She rarely came home before seven, often after eight. And that's when she wasn't out of town.

It was always the same, just as it was when he took his daughter to this park, always this park, Glencoe Park. So the image of their times together would be clearly and deeply etched into her memory as well as his own. That had been the plan, anyway. Even before the incident.

Now seeing the little girl swinging on the swing, and trying to remember his own daughter at that age, he realized it had all been to no avail. He felt depressed, much the same way he had when first arriving at the park an hour earlier. The picnic tables under the trees were the same, and that was heartening. But the moment he saw the play gym in the sand he knew he'd lost his hold on that part of their past. Everything was much smaller than he'd remembered, in relation to his daughter. She wasn't as excited as she was back then, either. She didn't take off running at the sight of the playground the way she used to. And that saddened him. He began to realize then that their day together wasn't going to be the way he had pictured it.

"I remember when you were her age," he said to his daughter, referring to the little girl who was now on the slide. Her mother still talking in low tones on the phone. "Sometimes when we were here at the park and I saw little six- and seven-year old girls, I'd try to imagine what it was going to be like when you were their age. I couldn't wait, you know, I was excited at the prospect. But no matter how hard I tried I could never imagine you being that old. Now that you are that old, I can't remember you as a four year old. Or even a five year old. No matter how hard I try, no matter how badly I want to go back, I can't seem to return to that time. Isn't that weird?"

His daughter continued to pump her legs, still not saying anything.

It was true. It had somehow slipped his mind. It was there one minute—clear as day—and then suddenly two years raced by and it was gone. Just like that.

———

It was awkward when he'd picked up his daughter earlier that day. It wasn't even noon yet and he knew he would have to convince the school to let his daughter leave with him.

The young woman at the front desk was frazzled. A temporary employee, she'd confessed, who seemed on the verge of walking out on the job. He could tell she was suspicious of him at first. She kept eyeing the ID badge on his shirt. So he told her he was an Army reservist. He said his medical unit was being deployed the following day, shipped overseas. When he told her that she immediately softened. She called him a patriot. She said she could understand how he would want to spend some quality time with his daughter. Then she was having his daughter paged on the intercom. A moment later there she was, coming down the hall in her little Catholic schoolgirl jumper. White leggings, a white blouse. Her long dark hair in a ponytail, a headband that matched the blue and green plaid of her uniform. Hush Puppies. For a moment he thought he would choke up and it took some effort to maintain his composure. The woman behind the desk was busy on the phone, hurriedly jotting down something on a legal pad, looking like she wanted to scream. He took his daughter aside and sat her in a chair where he could talk to her. She clearly wasn't expecting to see him and said she didn't want to leave school. But after a moment, and with the promise of burgers and ice cream—her idea—she agreed to leave with him.

After grabbing her coat and stocking cap from the peg outside her classroom, they got into the car and he told her they could do anything she wanted. That it was her special day. And he meant it. That had been his intention all along. He'd planned on doing whatever she wanted, even if it didn't entail Glencoe Park. Yet, suddenly, he felt himself wavering from that resolve. He realized he was hoping she would say she wanted to go to Glencoe Park, the way they used to. He noticed it was nearing noon, and he felt himself weakening as the old, irresistible impulses returned. He knew his daughter still lived in the same house and the park was right down the street. It's where they'd always gone together for lunch, so it was important they go there now. It was quickly becoming imperative. When she said she wanted to go downtown and to the aquarium he had to improvise. When he insisted they go to the park, for old time's sake, she wasn't mad exactly, but he could tell she was disappointed.

Then they were at the park with the bags of burgers and fries and sodas. She'd eaten her ice cream in the car on the way to the park. They sat down at a picnic table and her mood seemed to brighten. He wanted to test her memory and he said, "We used to have picnics here every day. At this very table, remember? I'd walk you over in the stroller and we'd have lunch. Just like we are now."

She took a small child's-bite of her burger, looking like she was trying to remember, and didn't say anything.

"Well?" he said, "Remember?"

She shook her head, nothing apparently coming to mind.

Now he wished he'd had the time earlier that morning to stop and buy a pail and shovel. Beach toys. He had the sudden urge to make sand cakes.

"And after that, we would dig in the sand," he said. He wanted to jog her memory, was sure he could. "Right over there." He pointed toward the sand under the far-reaching limb of an oak tree, offering the only shady spot in the sand, the only escape from the direct heat of the blistering sun on all those sweltering summer days they went there; the only shelter on the days it rained or sleeted. "We'd have a bucket and a shovel and we'd play in the sand, remember? Always in that same, exact spot. I would fill the bucket with sand and then turn it over to make sand cakes and you'd sit on them, as fast as I could build them. It was the funniest thing. I'd make ten sand cakes and you'd be giggling the whole time because we both knew you were only going to knock them down the second I had one built."

Tears rose up and momentarily blurred his vision as he laughed at the memory, though the picture of it was vague. Still, the memories he had that included his daughter's laughter were among his fondest. Her laughter, at least, was still clear in his mind, like music from a happier past.

She smiled at that, as if embarrassed by the story of herself as a baby, as if remembering.

"How 'bout that, Jules?" That ring a bell? Remember that?"

She chewed a large mouthful of burger and after a moment shook her head again, not seeming to remember.

———

They were in the car now and heading back home from the park. He was in no hurry to get there. He drove through the neighborhood as slowly as he could, following the same route he'd always taken when pushing his daughter in the stroller. But the feeling was lost, it wasn't the same. It was no good.

His daughter was buckled into the seat next to him. She wasn't saying anything. He had the heater on, running full blast, and she let the hot air wash over her cold, red hands. He didn't know what he'd expected, but he thought it would have been different. He was disappointed in himself. He had failed his daughter and himself. He honestly thought he'd changed, but now had to accept that perhaps he hadn't.

"I miss you, Jules," he said, suddenly feeling like he might break down. He found it difficult to talk. "Do you miss me, baby?" he added. "I mean, even a little?"

He could tell she was looking at him. She didn't seem to know what to say. He kept his eyes on the road because he couldn't bear to look at her. He took a deep, shaky breath to calm himself.

"Look," he said. "I'm sorry I've been away so long, baby. But it's not my fault. You have to understand that. I have no say in it."

She was still watching him, he could tell, and the silence was tearing him up inside.

He continued, the whole time struggling to maintain his composure, more than anything else, not wanting to look like some lunatic in front of his daughter.

"I don't mean to be this way, Jules, I swear," he said, and images from that day were suddenly running through his mind and he didn't want to look at them. His daughter on the swing, crying for him to stop pushing her. Him wanting to stop, but unable to—he wasn't finished counting yet. The swing going higher and higher until his daughter's little hands could no longer hold onto the chains. Still, it was freakish the way she fell to the sand. Kids fall all the time without getting hurt. She just happened to land awkwardly. It's what he'd explained to his wife at the emergency room. He would never purposely do anything to harm his own daughter. But none of that mattered to his wife. In her mind, that had been the last straw.

His daughter sniffled and he wondered if she were about to cry. He hoped he wasn't scaring her. It was important that she not be afraid of him.

"Look," he said. "No matter what happens, know that I love you. Okay, Jules? I've never stopped loving you. That's the important thing." He paused, again having to take a deep breath before continuing. "And, as long as I'm apologizing, let me say I'm sorry I made you go to the park today. I just wanted to have fun again the way we used to. That's all. God, I just want it back the way it used to be. I don't want to lose you, Jules. You can understand that, can't you?"

She still wasn't saying anything and now they were approaching the house; a little beige-brick Tudor with red and green trim. There was a squad car parked out front, city police. And now he knew what would happen. Sooner or later, he'd expected it.

He could see two policemen standing on the front porch. They were talking to his ex-wife who stood in the open doorway, wearing a dark blue business suit. Hugging herself against the cold. There was another man with them that he recognized from the clinic.

Then his daughter began talking.

"Daddy," she said. "Next time can we go to the aquarium?"

"Sure, baby," he said, still looking at his ex-wife. "I'm sorry we didn't go today like you wanted. I just thought you liked going to the park."

"I like the park, Daddy," she said and he knew she was telling the truth. Kids didn't lie, not like that. "But next time, could we go on the trolley like we used to? We could ride the trolley and go to the aquarium. We could eat Oreos and I could pull on the string and blow the horn. Right, Daddy?"

He rolled to a stop behind the police cruiser and shifted the car into park. His ex-wife looked at the car and didn't recognize it because it wasn't his. Her face was red and puffy. She'd been crying, that was obvious. Now she started to cry all over again as she recognized him behind the wheel, as she saw their daughter in the seat next to him. She pushed her way through the three men on the porch and began running toward the car, awkward in her high heels. Then the officers and the man turned and were following her.

His daughter was still talking. She said, "Daddy. Remember how we used to go on the trolley? I loved that."

She said it and he couldn't contain himself any longer. He wanted to look at his daughter and he did, at the same time, finally allowing himself to cry. She said it in a way that no daughter lost to her father ever could.

{11}

Rendezvous

After much speculation, it was agreed that Daphne Apodaca was of Mediterranean decent, maybe Asian. Steve secretly thought she was Polynesian, which may have had something to do with her hair, which hung straight down her back like a heavy swathe of black iridescent silk, reaching her waist without a single wave. The men talked of fantasies that had her feeding them grapes in Bedouin tents. Belly dancing, slowly and teasingly removing the layers of veils before expertly satisfying them. That she was versed in the ways of Kama Sutra was a given. Steve imagined himself on an island with her, maybe Tahiti. She was topless like in a Gaugin painting, palm trees and towering waterfalls in the background.

Steve wanted Daphne the first day he saw her, her first day on the job. So did the other men in the office, which was the way it was anytime a new, attractive girl started work. Daphne didn't appear to be as young as the other coordinators, she was maybe in her early thirties. Still, she was a good ten years younger than Steve. At the time, she'd been Jake Johnson's coordinator, the group creative director on the Golden Star Casinos account. He made a big deal of being her boss. Johnson knew the other men in the office always talked about

Daphne and he was often there, front and center, happily fueling the colorful discussions. Typically shy when it came to open talk about women, Steve would listen as the others worked themselves into a lather. Describing what they'd love to do to her, what they'd love for her to do to them.

Then, not a year later, Daphne was assigned to Steve after his promotion. He'd promptly taken over the Golden Star Casinos account after Jake Johnson was fired for disgracing himself and the agency. What exactly happened wasn't clear. Rumor had it that the pornography Johnson had downloaded onto his computer somehow made its way into a client presentation. To save face, and the twenty-five million dollar account, the agency's president supposedly made a show of canning Jake Johnson on the spot. Of course, none of that mattered to Steve. He was excited about the promotion, sure, but not as excited as he was to learn that Daphne Apodaca would be his new coordinator. He couldn't believe his good fortune, the way he might have felt if sitting on a plane and seeing her coming down the aisle. Incredulous that she, and not the tall, fat guy behind her, would take the seat next to his.

Daphne's voice matched her exotic look and sounded silky, like a whisper in a dream. Even now, hearing her say his name sent chills down Steve's inner thighs. One of the first things Steve did as her new boss was to have Daphne re-record his voicemail message. Sometimes he'd call himself just to hear her say his name. He found it dizzying.

Never in his life had a woman like Daphne had anything to do with him. He wasn't tall, fit, or athletic, never had been, so he'd accepted his place farther down the alpha-ladder. He'd felt lucky marrying his wife, and she was no looker. So in the beginning, Steve naturally didn't dare talk to Daphne unless it was to request his schedule or to have her make travel arrangements. Keeping it strictly official. Still, as his coordinator, Daphne had to talk to him and after a while Steve began baiting her with conversation. He'd soon discovered the uptown neighborhood where she lived alone. She always had a Jumpin' Java coffee cup on her desk so he knew she stopped for coffee on the way into work every morning, same as he did. They had that in common and he made a note of it.

Early one Saturday morning Steve found himself driving into the city from his suburban home. He'd had the urge to drive around uptown, acting on a plan he was scarcely conscious of. He saw that there were several Jumpin' Javas in uptown and a couple more between there and the office building where the agency was located downtown. Then the plan became clear in his mind. Beginning that next Monday, he went to a different one of these Jumpin' Javas early each morning until he saw Daphne come in. As she moved coolly through the café in her high heels, heads rose from newspapers, laptops, and espresso drinks. Both men and women watching her, it was no different than it was at the office. Steve decided to walk up to the condiment counter for a packet of Sweet and Low. He never added anything to his coffee, but on this morning he added the sweetener to his Americano and that's how he ran into her. She seemed surprised to see him, no less surprised as he acted to see her. It turned out she lived in the apartments above the café. He invited her to join him, which she did. Then the awkwardness and stiff superficial talk they'd had at the office slowly gave way to real conversation. They talked more in an hour than they had in the previous three months. He knew he wasn't funny, even for an advertising creative. Still, she laughed at everything he said, and that was soon another of the many things he found so intoxicating about her.

Then she was running into him at this same café on many

of the following mornings. Each time acting as surprised as the first time she'd run into him. Two months later, they were meeting every day, two hours before work. Even though they had little in common, except for the fact that she was his co-ordinator, he was her boss, and the sex they were having each morning.

———

Daphne had a habit of rubbing lotion on her hands, as casually as other women might apply lip balm. The lotion had an exotic aromatic coconut butter smell to it that Steve immediately associated with her, which only added to his Tahitian fantasy.

"Those have to be the luckiest hands on the planet," he told Daphne one morning. Without stopping, she looked down at her hands and studied them rubbing lotion on one another. She then looked at Steve with a playful smile.

"Let me see your hands," she said. After squirting more lotion into the palm of her hand, she began expertly massaging his fingers, one at a time. It was the most incredible thing he'd ever felt. Conscious of everyone around him, he felt embarrassed, yet, at the same time, glad they were watching this young, exotic woman massaging his hands. Then this too became a part of the routine. Later in the day, he would hold his hands to his face while seated at his desk, breathing in deeply, as if breathing her in. He wished the men at his office could see it, knowing they'd be no less envious as the men sitting in the chairs around him at the café. No less envious as the men in his office had been of Jake Johnson when he was Daphne's boss.

———

"So, why me?" Steve asked.

"What do you mean?" Daphne said, looking like she really didn't understand what he meant. They sat together on the sofa at the café.

"You know. Of all the guys in the office, I'm the one you're with."

He'd asked her this once before when they were in bed. She told him she liked that he wasn't like the other men in the office, who had all hit on her. She liked that he was quiet. Shy seeming, yet in a position of power. It was a real turn-on, she said. Hearing this, Steve realized that, in that moment, Daphne had made a lifetime of being unremarkable worth it.

"I can't explain it, Daph," he said. "Women like you aren't supposed to be with guys like me. I mean you were with Jake Johnson."

"Oh, my God," she said, her voice suddenly rising as a change came over her. "Don't even mention that asshole."

"Sorry, Daphne," Steve said, talking in a low voice, trying to calm her down. He looked around the café to see if anyone was watching. "I guess I didn't realize it ended so badly for you two."

Then Daphne smiled and Steve thought it odd, maniacal, even, the way her anger turned to what now appeared to be rapture. "It ended worse for him than it did me, okay," she said.

"Okay."

Steve wasn't going to pursue it. He wanted to steer the conversation back to where it had started. When she was about to tell him how special he was as a man.

"You still don't understand what happened to him, do you?" she said. "Nobody does."

"What do you mean?" Steve wanted her to lower her voice.

"In that client meeting," she said. "How it all went wrong."

"I heard he screwed up the power point presentation or something. But no one's saying anything. No one seems to know anything more than that."

"Screwed it up?" Daphne said, her voice rising again. "That's an understatement."

"How do you know all this?" Steve said. "Did he tell you what happened?"

"Let's just say the images in the presentation were not the ones he'd intended to use."

"What?"

"I wish I could've been there to see it," she said. "At least the client got to see the kind of pig they were working with. They got to see the man I knew."

A moment passed and then, just like that, Daphne was herself again. No longer seeming insane.

"Anyway," she said, "you're nothing like him. And that's what I love about you. You aren't full of yourself. I swear, I'm through with guys like Jake Johnson screwing me over."

———

They lay in bed holding each other and not saying anything after it was over. Steve thought of his wife. He reminded himself that she never drove into the city. She rarely left the house all day, and that was in Frisco, twenty-five miles away. But there was always a chance she might drop by out of the blue, and he was beginning to get paranoid.

Still, Steve couldn't seem to stop the affair. The thought of getting deeper into the relationship scared the hell out of him, yet he knew it would have to go a lot deeper before it ended. Funny how he couldn't wait to get Daphne into bed each morning. Little else occupied his mind from the moment he woke up and set out on the drive into the city. Then when it was over and they were lying there beneath the sheets, his mind was instantly focused on getting dressed and out of her apartment.

———

Steve told Daphne a lie. Or what he knew was probably a lie. And because he'd never stopped her from building on that initial lie, it was now understood that he would soon be leaving his wife. On the surface, it felt like a doable thing, sitting in the café as Daphne massaged his hands. But the more Daphne talked about it, the more Steve thought about what all leaving his wife would entail. Alimony. Lawyers. The shame. And now Daphne clung to the idea, bringing it up every chance she got.

One morning before work, they were lying in bed after it was over. Her long, red manicured nails raking up and down his stomach in a way that had at one time aroused him to his core. That now only reminded him of how deep into it he was.

"What are you thinking?" Daphne said.

Steve thought of the three storyboards that were due that day. He thought how he wanted to fire one of his junior art directors. He thought of the office and how he could be at his desk in twenty minutes if he got up now, got dressed and left. But he didn't say any of that. Instead, he said, "I'm not thinking anything."

"I hate that your mind is always preoccupied with how unhappy you are," Daphne said. "With your wife, I mean."

"There's nothing you can do about it," he said.

"I'm your coordinator," she said. "It's my job to make you happy."

"You want to make me happy?"

"You know I do," she said, sitting up with a growing, mischievous smile. She straddled him, waiting for him to tell her how she could make him happy.

"I've got to get my Christmas cards out. My wife won't leave me alone about it. How 'bout I put you in charge of that. It'd mean the world to me, Daph."

A look of disappointment replaced Daphne's smile. Then she became playful again. "You sure that's all I can do to make you happy?" she said.

———

Two weeks before Thanksgiving, and the café was already decorated for Christmas—green bunting, and shiny red ornaments throughout. A life size cardboard Santa holding a Jumpin' Java cup. Pre-wrapped Christmas gift-boxes featuring coffee mugs, coffee beans and chocolate. Bing Crosby sang White Christmas. Steve loathed this time of year. The lies, the deception, the all out marketing blitzes.

Steve and Daphne sat at the café talking in hushed tones, as she massaged his hand. Suddenly, a barista approached their sofa; an effeminate little man with a tongue stud wearing a Santa hat. He pointed a Polaroid camera at them. Before Steve could refuse, Daphne leaned in toward him, smiling. After taking the picture, the barista inserted the Polaroid into a cardboard frame that was red and decorated with wreaths of holly and Jumpin' Java logos made to look like snowflakes.

"Can I have it," Daphne said, eager to see the picture materialize.

"Of course," Steve said, for some reason thinking he would've thrown the picture away.

"Bet it would make a nice Christmas card," Daphne said, handling the picture carefully with two lotion-slick fingertips. "Don't you think?"

She waited for an answer. Steve could tell by the way she looked at him that she would weigh his response. She did it all the time now and Steve was always careful not to piss her off. Daphne didn't hurt easily, he'd come to realize. She didn't seem to wound. She just got mad, and that scared him.

"I don't know, Daph," Steve said. "Not this year, okay?"

"I know that, silly," she said. "But maybe next year?"

"Okay," he said, regretting he'd said it.

"You promise?"

Steve didn't see the harm in promising. A year was a long time. A lot could happen.

"Okay, I promise," he said.

"Promise what?"

"I promise it'll be a picture of us on the Christmas card next year."

That seemed to satisfy her, as she returned her attention to his hand. Stroking his fingers as if coaxing milk from a goat's teat. A promise of what was to come once back in her bedroom and she had his pants off, the same bottle of aromatic lotion on the nightstand.

———

The next day, Steve saw the Polaroid when he glanced into Daphne's cubicle. She'd pinned it to the wall next to a mix of other photos already there. Pictures of Daphne and what Steve assumed was her father; Daphne and her cat; Daphne and groups of girl friends; another with someone as exotic as she was, maybe her mother, maybe her sister. Steve didn't know what to think. He decided not to say anything, not letting Daphne know he saw it.

After that he couldn't pass by her cubicle without glancing

in to look at the photo. The look on his face, the look on hers, their lotion-slick hands intertwined and frolicking. He wondered who else in the office had seen it.

———

"So what happened to the picture, Steve?" Daphne said, standing in Steve's office doorway.

The next morning, Steve had decided against going to the café. Instead, he'd gone straight to the office and was now at his desk working at his computer.

"What picture?" he said, trying to think of something to say.

"You know what picture," she said. "Don't treat me like an idiot. What'd you do with it?"

"What?" Steve said.

"I know it was you who took it," she said.

Steve now saw the side of Daphne that frightened him. "Daphne, I don't know what you're talking about," he said. "Now if you'll excuse me, I have a ton of work to do."

"You don't know what happened to the picture from Jumpin' Java?" she said.

Steve could tell he had her wavering. She wouldn't have asked him that if she knew for sure.

"Oh, that picture," he said. "The last time I saw it was on your . . ." and here he realized what he was saying aloud. Lowering his voice to a whisper, he continued, ". . . it was on your bedside table. That's where you'd put it after that guy took our picture." It was partly true. Steve remembered it there on the table, facing the bed as they had sex. He couldn't stop looking at it, as much as he'd tried.

Daphne didn't say anything. She stood there looking like she might scream. He could see behind her, the activity in the office. No one seemed to notice what was going on and he was relieved.

"You're such a fucking asshole," Daphne said. "First you blow me off this morning, and then you steal my picture." She paused and Steve could see the tension building within her. He could feel the tension building within himself. "You didn't have to act like this," she continued. "We could have talked it over. You only had to be honest with me. But you're a coward, just like Jake Johnson. Well if that's the way you want it, fine."

Then she turned and stomped off toward her cubicle, her hair flowing behind her with the fluidity and luster of a satin veil.

———

That seemed to be the end of it. Still, Steve waited. He couldn't help dreading the revenge that he was sure was coming.

But time passed and nothing happened. Daphne still did her job as professionally as before. She acted toward Steve the way she had before the morning meetings at the café. When he'd wanted her and she didn't seem to know he existed beyond being her boss. She acted coldly, but he could accept that now. Then almost a year passed and it was nearing Christmas.

"I took care of the Christmas cards the way you asked me to," Daphne said. She'd walked into Steve's office and now stood there holding one of the cards.

Steve looked up from his computer. "Thanks again, Daphne, for taking that off my plate again this year," he said. "Now if I can only find time to mail them."

"I hope you don't mind, but I already took care of it," she

said.

"You mean you mailed them already?" he said.

"All seventy-four of them," she said.

Steve had wanted to look at the cards one last time before mailing them off. It was in his nature. As a group creative director, nothing went out without his approval. But then, he thought, it would be a good gesture to show Daphne he trusted her. She no longer seemed to harbor any bad feelings, and he thought she deserved it.

"I appreciate that, Daphne," he said. "I know I say it every year, but next year I'm going to get them done early. I swear the holidays seem to ambush me every time."

"Anyway, there was one left over," Daphne said.

Again, Steve noticed the card she was holding.

"So I hoped you wouldn't mind if I kept it for myself."

"No, Daphne, I don't mind at all," he said, amazed. It'd taken a long time, nearly a year, but she seemed her old self again and Steve was glad for it. "Actually . . ." he started to say.

"What?" she said.

"Well, to tell you the truth, I'm really glad to see you wanting to keep it."

She's incredible, Steve thought. She really was taking it better than he would have. She obviously didn't feel anything for him anymore, and he realized he wasn't happy the way he thought he would be if ever seeing her no longer in love with him. Maybe he'd misjudged her. Maybe they could start over. Maybe after the New Year he'd start going to Jumpin' Java again. For old time's sake. See what might happen.

Steve couldn't help looking at the Christmas card in Daphne's hand. He caught glimpses of it as she talked, waving it around as she gestured.

"Great," she said. "Now I only have to decide where to put it."

A dizzying wave rushed over Steve as he recognized the photograph.

"I mean I could put it in my office," she continued, "but someone might steal it like they did the original."

Steve didn't say anything. Daphne held the card steady now so he could see the picture clearly. It was of a poor quality. Grainy, as any reproduction of a Polaroid will be. But it was clear enough and his eyes moved over the picture of him sitting next to Daphne at the café. The terror on his face, the triumphant smile on hers, much the way they looked now here in his office. He looked a long time at his lotion-slick hand in hers and felt he might vomit, as he caught a hint of the familiar aromatic coconut butter smell.

{12}

The Way You Really Are?

Spying on people wasn't what Luke LaCroix had in mind when first climbing the old magnolia. Once at the top of the tree, he was taken with the panoramic view of the bayou and the surrounding yards. Even more, there was the sudden fascination of simple every day occurrences: A tugboat pushing a gravel-laden barge down river. His dog gnawing on a soup bone. Even something as mundane as the occasional car driving up or down Eleazar Street somehow struck Luke as interesting in a way that seeing it from ground level didn't. He found that if he sat up in the tree long enough, the animals didn't notice him anymore. A cardinal nearly landed at the top of the tree one day before being startled at the sudden sight of Luke crouched there in the branches. It'd changed direction in mid-flight in such a way that had Luke thinking for a second that the bird might actually have a heart attack and drop straight from the sky.

But it was watching people that intrigued Luke most. Like seeing Mrs. Bergeron through his binoculars, walking to the mailbox at the end of her driveway. Never without her cigarette case in the event she ran into Mrs. Dubois and ended up stuck in long conversation; seeing his uncle Jules out in the driveway working on his boat, whistling; his grandmother's maid, Lucille, hanging sheets on the clothesline, slow and methodical; Kenny Meaux outside with his little dog, washing and waxing his sports car. It was Luke's discovery of the Broussards in particular, though, that caught Luke's interest. They lived next door. Not that Ruth and Albert Broussard ever did anything out of the ordinary. In fact, the first few times spying on them were uneventful.

Miss Ruth, as everyone called her, was always working in one of the many flowerbeds, while talking to the plants and flowers. She talked to the birds, too. She might encourage the begonias with a pep talk. She spoke to a hydrangea bush, as if addressing a baby in a bassinette; berating the pansies for appearing sick and not blooming to their potential, while praising the miniature roses for displaying an abundance of new growth. Then she would raise her voice, scolding the coco grass for growing amid her zinnias, for crowding out the day lilies. "You don't belong here!" she'd say to the weeds, pulling them from the soil one at a time. "You keep out."

It wasn't unusual for Luke to see Miss Ruth talking to the plants and the birds, even when he wasn't in the tree and the old lady could see him and knew he could hear her. It wasn't unusual to see her cursing the chicken snakes that shimmied up the pole of her Purple Martin house, or the crows for having the audacity to fly over her yard. Still, it made Luke laugh. Because when hidden from Miss Ruth, he knew she didn't know he was watching her, and that somehow made it different.

Albert Broussard would also be out working in the yard. Always wearing long khaki pants and a matching long sleeve shirt that would be soaked through with perspiration. Wearing a handkerchief under his broad-billed cap so that it draped over his neck in a way that reminded Luke of French Foreign

Legion movies. Mr. Albert wasn't only allergic to bees and wasps, but also to the sun.

For as long as Luke could remember, the Broussards had always been nice to him. They had always let Luke pick oranges and cumquats and pears from their trees. Or pomegranates. They encouraged him to. If she'd baked cookies, Miss Ruth would call to Luke across the hurricane fence when she saw him in the yard, inviting him into their house. She'd say he was too skinny. Then she'd sit him down with a tall glass of cold milk and all the cookies he could eat. She was like a grandmother in that way. But that was before Luke had discovered that the Broussards only acted nice because they didn't know he knew better.

———

That it wasn't limited to the Broussards was maybe the single most profound revelation of Luke's life. Up until he was ten, anyway, because that's when he'd first seen the same thing with the Heberts.

Luke wasn't sure when they'd become friends exactly, but his parents were suddenly doing things with the Heberts all the time. And that was fine with Luke, because the Heberts had two daughters. Nicole, who was Luke's age, and Collette, who was a year older. Both were blonde, both had coal-black eyes, and both were beautiful. Sometimes Luke would go with his family to the Heberts' house on weekends. A big sprawling estate outside of town with a pool and a lot of horses. Or the Heberts would come to Luke's house for dinner and the adults would get drunk and play bourré and laugh loudly. Meanwhile, Luke and the two girls played together. Luke envied the Heberts. They were rich. They had a large house, a big Sedan de Ville Cadillac, two beautiful daughters, and a swimming pool. He couldn't help sometimes wishing his family were more like the Heberts.

One Sunday, they were at the Heberts' house swimming and barbequing. Just the same old thing. It was fun and Luke was feeling envious of the Heberts. He had gone inside the house to use the bathroom, just off the kitchen. Luke could see the pool from the bathroom window and he watched Nicole and Collette, both basking in the sun on towels and glistening with coconut oil. Suddenly he heard the sliding glass door that led out to the pool. It opened and closed, and then someone was in the kitchen. Luke froze, not making a sound. The freezer door opened and he could hear ice cubes falling into a glass. Moments later, the sliding door opened once more and closed and Luke was about to exit the bathroom. He thought he was alone in the house again. As he reached for the knob, he heard Mr. Hebert say something. It was in a harsh tone and Luke almost didn't recognize him. Mrs. Hebert said something back, sounding just as hateful. Then they were both going at it, shouting and cussing and Luke knew they didn't know he was in the bathroom. He remained frozen. He was afraid to come out of the bathroom and he waited for Mr. and Mrs. Hebert to leave. Then they both stopped screaming at each other at the same time. Luke heard them whispering. All at once, the door to the bathroom swung open and Mr. and Mrs. Hebert were standing there looking at him, their faces blank. They still seemed drunk, but not in the happy way they usually were. The way they'd been moments earlier out at the pool. They didn't say anything. Then they both smiled and had become the Heberts he'd known before they'd come into the kitchen to get ice and scream at each other, no longer acting the way they really were.

———

It got so that Luke began wondering about everyone. Even his parents, although he'd never witnessed anything from the tree or anywhere else to warrant such thinking. He might see his mom come out of the house, get into the car and drive off. It was exciting, knowing she didn't know he was watching her. Or Luke might see his father come home in the evening before letting the Labs out of the kennel to run. Luke's father would talk to the dogs affectionately, but that wasn't unusual. He did that even when he knew Luke was watching. Still, Luke thought he might have detected a difference in his father's demeanor, he couldn't be sure.

Luke knew from experience that catching people being the way they really are didn't happen right away. You had to wait for it and Luke was sure if he watched long enough, sooner or later he would see something, even in his parents. It frightened him to think what he might see.

———

It'd taken a while for something to happen with the Broussards. Then one day, something did happen. Luke sat crouched in the tree, not expecting to see what he would see. Miss Ruth, on her knees in the flowerbed, talked to the flowers and plants and it was funny the way it always was. As she dug in the dirt with a metal hand claw, Mr. Albert came from the front of the house, pushing a wheelbarrow loaded with leaves and sticks, moving toward the bayou. As he passed his wife, Mr. Albert pushed the wheelbarrow over the small piles of weeds she'd discarded. Miss Ruth didn't start yelling at her husband until he was well past her.

"So you're just gonna leave that there for me to pick up,

uh?" she said, referring to the bunches of weeds she'd pulled. "Well, you're just plain goddamn selfish, that's what you are?"

She yelled at Mr. Albert as if yelling at a crow or a chicken snake, one of the many things she detested and at which she was always cursing.

"Pick it up your goddamn self," Mr. Albert said, sounding just as malicious. He continued moving toward the bayou, mumbling something to himself.

"Selfish!" Miss Ruth shrieked.

Luke found it disturbing, the way she sounded. She didn't sound like herself. She sounded crazy.

Miss Ruth stood up. She continued shouting, still shrieking insane-like. "Selfish! Selfish!" She threw the hand claw at her husband and hit him squarely in the back of the head. He instantly brought a hand up toward his head and the wheelbarrow rolled over, spilling its contents. Mr. Albert appeared stunned. Then he picked up the hand claw. He turned and faced his wife. After standing there for a moment, he threw the hand claw as hard as an old man can, just missing his wife's face. Miss Ruth shrieked something unintelligible and didn't move, holding her ground. Mr. Albert had taken a handkerchief from his pocket. He had it pressed against his head. He stood there a long time, staring back at his wife.

High up in the branches of the magnolia, Luke's backside was going numb. His foot had fallen asleep. He'd been in the tree a good while. He reminded himself that he was getting too big to be climbing that high up. The top of the tree trembled, then dipped slightly, as he repositioned himself. That's when Luke heard Miss Ruth, and he knew she wasn't screaming at Mr. Albert or the coco grass.

"Mother of God," she said. "Boy, what the hell are you doin' up there?"

That's when things changed between Luke and the Broussards for good. After that, when Luke saw the Broussards in the yard and they saw him, it didn't matter. Now if Luke ever came upon the old couple in the middle of an argument, they'd keep at it. Or else they'd direct their hate toward him, because they knew he knew and there was no point in pretending anymore. Climbing the old magnolia suddenly made no sense to Luke. It had become clear that he didn't have to be in a tree to see people acting the way they really are.

{13}

Feliz Cumpleaños

Lupé's little girl, Regina, was having a birthday party. Lupé felt obligated to invite the Turners' little boy, whose name was Michael. The two kids played together on Fridays, the one day Lupé was permitted to bring her daughter with her to the Turners' house. Lupé was Michael's full-time nanny.

As Lupé sat at the counter in the kitchen addressing her daughter's party invitations, Mrs. Turner walked in and saw them spread out across the table. Lupé had thought Mrs. Turner was upstairs getting dressed. She wondered if Mrs. Turner might give her a cold look for spending her time on the invitations and not the silver she was supposed to be polishing. Instead, Mrs. Turner smiled. "Oh, little Regina's having a birthday party," she said. "How fun!"

Feeling put on the spot, Lupé added Michael's name to an envelope. She left his invitation in the mailbox on the way out the door that evening. Never thinking for a minute that the Turners would actually take their son to her daughter's birthday party.

So it was with some surprise when the Turners did show up at the party. Lupé and her friends, who also worked as nannies or maids, often talked about their employers. About the peculiar things they did, their often strange habits—how they were bossy or condescending. But now Lupé was made to realize that she'd had her employers all wrong. Maybe the Turners were different. There was no doubting the pride she felt seeing the Turners arrive at her daughter's party. Lupé could hardly contain herself. She beamed as she helped Michael from his car seat, hoisting him up and into her arms. She proudly carried him to the patio where her girlfriends sat at the picnic table, showing him off as if he were her own child. Lupé's girlfriends made a spectacle of gushing over the little boy. Many of them worked for families in the same neighborhood where the Turners lived. As the Turners pulled up in their big, white Mercedes Lupé could tell by the stunned look on her friends' faces that they were jealous. She knew what they were thinking: Never in a million years would their employers think of coming to their kids' birthday parties.

Being the only Anglos at the party—they were the only Anglos invited—the Turners looked awkward and out of place. A tall, pale man, Mr. Turner smiled a lot, showing his large, white and even teeth. He chose to sit with the women at one of the tables under a big umbrella, and not with the men who stood huddled around the barbeque pit drinking beer. He wore white linen shorts, leather sandals, and a colorful shirt he'd brought back from their trip to Hawaii. A shirt Lupé had pressed and starched only the week before.

Mr. Turner wasn't using his Spanish the way he did with Lupé at the house. He always tried a new line on her as he grabbed a cup of coffee on his way out the door. He might say, "El café es muy rico." Or "Hace mucho calor hoy." To this, Lupé always laughed, clapping her hands. Saying "very good, Mr. Turner!" Then she would continue, not in her broken English, but in Spanish. Saying that, yes, the coffee was rich.

Or that, it was true, the weather was very hot that day. She was always eager to continue the conversation. But the moment Lupé would say anything in return, speaking Spanish as slowly and as clearly as she could—as slowly as Mr. Turner spoke Spanish—his jovial expression would vanish, a look of embarrassment reddening his pale complexion in splotches. Then he'd laugh awkwardly before leaving.

Mrs. Turner, on the other hand, seemed comfortable at the party. She talked a lot and to everyone. Also in English and not Spanish. Some of Lupé's friends didn't speak English. Those that could didn't speak it well enough to hold a conversation with Mrs. Turner, who talked rapidly. Appearing more gracious than Lupé had ever seen her, she looked radiant in her bright yellow sundress, and the kinds of sandals that had long leather straps looping many times around her tanned ankles and calves. An outfit Lupé had never seen before. Mrs. Turner looked truly elegant and Lupé couldn't help feeling flattered, knowing that Mrs. Turner had put some thought into what she chose to wear for the party. But then, Mrs. Turner took great care in selecting anything she wore, even if for just milling around the house.

Just in case they did come to the party, Lupé had bought a six-pack of Heineken. She knew Mr. Turner drank that brand because there were always empty Heineken bottles in the garbage. Lupé knew Mrs. Turner preferred wine because she was usually walking around the house with a glass by four or five o'clock. While Lupé couldn't find Mrs. Turner's label, she did know it was white wine. So Lupé had settled on a twelve dollar bottle, careful to remove the price tag, the way she'd done with the Heineken. She didn't want her husband to see how much she'd spent.

It made Lupé happy seeing Mr. Turner drinking a Heineken. She hoped he felt more at home because of it; more at home than he looked, anyway. Lupé had never seen Mr. Turner frightened before, but thought that might be the way he looked now. Mrs. Turner drank the wine that Lupé had given her, sipping it from a paper party cup that had colorful balloons on it. Lupé felt happy that the Turners were there. She was glad most of her friends were accepting of the couple, even if not talking to them very much.

Everything appeared perfect, Lupé thought as she surveyed the party from the top of the steps at the backdoor. As she exited the house with a large aluminum pan of charro beans, she glanced toward the swing set and saw that the Turner boy was having a good time. He stood out among the other children, much like his father did at the picnic tables. Initially, this had Lupé feeling anxious, thinking the Turners saw the same thing. If they noticed the difference, Lupé couldn't tell.

The other children didn't seem to notice the difference either, welcoming the little blond, rosy-cheeked boy—a smaller version of his father. Lupé's daughter and the other children led him to the bounce house, helping him remove his shoes. They showed him how to hold the sawed-off broom handle before letting him stand first in line when the time came for the piñata.

Lupé had spent the week before the party readying her house. It was cleaner even than usual. So when Mrs. Turner finally asked to use the restroom, Lupé was happy to show her where it was. She'd hoped Mrs. Turner would notice the lamp she'd allowed Lupé to take from a box in the garage filled with things destined for the Salvation Army. Following Lupé through the house, Mrs. Turner did notice the lamp in the living room. She said it looked divine. She joked that maybe she'd have to ask for it back. They laughed together in a way they never would have at the Turners' house.

———

Michael's birthday was a month after Regina's, and Mrs. Turner began planning for it immediately. Coming home with shopping bags one day, Mrs. Turner showed Lupé the party napkins and plates she'd bought, as if seeking her opinion. Lupé thought they were very nice and she said so. Mrs. Turner inquired about the piñata that had been at Regina's party. She said she might get one too, it looked like such fun. Mrs. Turner showed Lupé a picture of the cake she'd ordered; an enormous cake with an entire barnyard on it, complete with cows, horses, pigs, chickens, even a red barn. They didn't make cakes like that at the grocery store where Lupé had bought her daughter's cake.

Lupé wanted to buy Michael something special for his birthday, but couldn't think of anything. Then one day, as she walked the boy through the neighborhood in the stroller, a fire truck approached. It came barreling down the street, its sirens wailing, horn blasting, and lights flashing. When Lupé bent down into the stroller, she expected to find the boy crying hysterically. What she saw in his eyes, though, wasn't terror, but exhilaration. He was laughing his little boy laugh and, all at once, Lupé knew what she would get him for his birthday.

Lupé helped Mrs. Turner put together the party favors. Filling the decorative bags with candy, kazoos, water pistols and little plastic barnyard animals like the ones on the cake in the picture. Lupé helped stuff the envelopes with invitations. When she didn't see her daughter's name on any of them, she told herself that Mrs. Turner wouldn't be mailing Regina's invitation. Instead, she would likely hand it to Lupé one day as she left for home at the end of the day. Or maybe Mrs. Turner was waiting for a Friday, when Michael could then personally present the invitation to Regina. The image of the little boy handing her daughter an invitation nearly brought Lupé to tears.

On the week of the party Mrs. Turner asked Lupé if her family had plans that Saturday, the day of the party. Lupé said no, not that she knew of. Then Mrs. Turner asked if Lupé could work that day, to help keep an eye on Michael and the other children and to help clean up after the party. There was no mention of Regina's name and then Lupé knew for sure. Still, Lupé said yes. Of course, she would be happy to be a part of Michael's party. She'd already bought him the toy fire truck.

{14}

Trawling

Suddenly, the engines screamed as the boat jerked violently to a stop, and everyone was thrown forward. Now the boat seemed to be going in reverse as the swell they'd just climbed over caught up with them and crashed into the stern. Water poured over the back of the boat.

"Dad!" Luke LaCroix shouted. His tennis shoes squeaked on the wet deck as he kept himself from falling. He was sure they were sinking.

Luke's father picked himself up off the deck where he'd fallen hard. Before he could make his way back to the helm, another swell caught up to the boat and crashed over the stern. The white picnic basket at the back of the boat was half under water and soaked.

"Tommy, shut it down!" Mr. Sonnier shouted over the high-pitched strain of the engines. He'd dropped his paperback book in the excitement and it was now floating pages-open in the water. Mr. Sonnier braced his tall, heavy body against the slant of the boat. Luke's father cut the wheel before idling the engines. With the stern no longer into the oncoming swell, the water wasn't pouring into the boat anymore.

"What are we gonna do?" Luke said. He was terrified at the

thought of sinking.

"Mais, everything's gonna be okay, T-Luke," Mr. Sonnier said. "It's gonna be awright, boy."

The wide-bodied twenty-five-foot Bertram sat level on the water now, the broad swell rolling under the boat. The half-foot of water in the stern began draining, the paperback slowly spiraling in a small eddy over the drain grate. The trawl lines no longer trailed behind them, but instead slanted off to the side, taut against the pull of the boat. Luke's father tugged on one of the ropes like he expected to pull what the boat couldn't. After a moment he gave up red-faced. "Goddammit," he shouted.

Mr. Sonnier held his big, doughy chin in his large hand. "Mais, whatcha think it is, huh, Tommy?" he said.

"It's snagged, that's what it is," Luke's father said. "Brand new goddamn net, too."

"Let's back up and pull in as much line as we can," Mr. Sonnier said. "Maybe we can unsnag it from another angle. I can't imagine what it is, but maybe we can work it loose." Mr. Sonnier talked in a voice that calmed Luke. He was taking control and it seemed to settle down Luke's father, just as he was about to explode. Luke was glad Mr. Sonnier was there.

Luke hadn't always been happy having Mr. Sonnier along. Luke wasn't sure why, but in the beginning he didn't like Mr. Sonnier. He didn't like it when Mr. Sonnier started going trawling with them. Mr. Sonnier was different than his father's other fishing friends, the ones that had gone trawling with them in the past. It was different back then. When they'd roughed it on the boat, eating stale saltines and sardines, potted meat and Vienna sausages for lunch; what Luke considered man's food. But over time Luke had accepted Mr. Sonnier and the extravagant lunches he always packed for everyone—chicken salad, boudin balls, deviled eggs, fruit cocktail, French bread, homemade brownies. Even etouffe once. What Luke couldn't get used to, though, was the enormous white picnic basket in which Mr. Sonnier packed everything. Luke's father teased Mr. Sonnier about the basket, seeming to feel the same way about it as Luke. It always embarrassed Luke, having to load the basket onto the boat at the marina, along with the other things you'd expect to see men load on board a boat. Like the several ice chests, the trawl net and its two heavy wooden boards, tackle boxes, rods and reels—the things men were expected to use on a boat.

Now Luke's father stood at the stern, a hand shielding his eyes from the glare. He'd calmed down. "There aren't any reefs off Redfish Point," he said. "Are there, Sonny?"

Luke's father looked out toward land, at the small peninsula of marsh that jutted out into the gulf like a bridge connecting to nowhere. Then he looked out at the water off the port side and at the two trawl lines that dipped at an angle into the water.

"Mais, look at that, even the float's under water," Mr. Sonnier said. The gallon milk jug tied to the trail line was no longer afloat. "It doesn't get that deep here, uh?"

"It's not supposed to be more than ten to twelve feet," Luke's father said. "Hell, I should know, I've trawled here enough."

"Maybe the net's full and the boat can't pull it anymore," Luke said.

Luke's father and Mr. Sonnier looked at Luke. They didn't know what he was talking about.

Luke said, "Remember that time Mr. Broussard told us how someone he knew hit a school of shrimp?"

Luke envisioned the net filled with shrimp. The idea had him excited.

"Oh, no Luke, I don't think that's what it is, son," Luke's

father said, almost laughing; seeming to have forgotten how mad he was that his new sixteen-foot trawl net was snagged on something down at the bottom of the Gulf. "God, I wish that's what it was, but I'm afraid the net's just hung up on something."

"Mais, I don't know, Tommy," Mr. Sonnier said. "T-Luke might be onto somethin', uh."

"Sonny, c'mon," Luke's father said. "You're both dreaming."

"Well, then we just gonna have to see, won't we?" Mr. Sonnier said, giving Luke a wink.

They'd pulled in the ropes as much as they could and then motored around the area in a tight circle, trying to work the net free. Still, the net remained anchored solidly.

"Damn thing is stuck for good," Luke's father said.

"Talk about," Mr. Sonnier said.

"So whatcha think?"

"Well, Tommy, I know it's not what you wanna hear," Mr. Sonnier said, "but I think we gonna have to leave it here."

"No way, Sonny. We're not cutting the ropes." Luke's father said, upset again. "That's a brand new net. I just got it."

"Then we gonna have to dive for it," Mr. Sonnier said, like he'd saved the idea and now it was the only thing left to say. "I figure if we follow the ropes down we bound to find out what it's hung up on. If we can't un-snag it, we can always cut it loose."

Luke could tell by watching his father that the idea made a lot of sense. "I think we can move the boat a little closer," his father said. "That'll allow us a straighter dive down."

"I figure that'd put us about right there," Mr. Sonnier said, pointing to a spot on the water.

Luke looked on with interest as the two men continued talking. He wondered if they would strip down or if they would make the dive with their clothes on. He wondered what Mr. Sonnier would look like in his underwear.

Luke's father maneuvered the boat over the spot where they'd decided the net was snagged and now the two trawl lines angled straight down into the water. Luke's father turned the bow into the swell, holding the position.

Luke wanted to help. He wanted his father to know he wanted to help, but there wasn't anything for him to do. After a while, his father and Mr. Sonnier seemed to finally have it all figured out.

"Luke," his father said. "We need to talk."

Luke felt something was wrong. He knew what his father was about to say.

"Please don't make me do it, dad," Luke said. The thought of swimming in the Gulf, where he'd caught sharks, scared him.

"Son, there's no other way. Do you have any suggestions, because I don't know what else to do." His father looked toward the bow where Mr. Sonnier was lowering the anchor to hold the boat steady and in line with the oncoming swell. Luke could tell his father didn't want Mr. Sonnier to hear what he was about to say. "Can you picture that big clumsy coon-ass swimming around down there?"

Luke had already imagined it. He'd laughed at the idea. But now it wasn't funny. "Couldn't we just pull on it some more with the boat?" he said, knowing as he said it that it would anger his father.

"Luke, we've pulled on it already," his father said, his voice rising. "You saw us pull on it, didn't you? It's stuck."

Luke could see Mr. Sonnier moving toward them from the bow along the narrow starboard walkway, careful on the wet decking.

"Dang, Tommy," Mr. Sonnier said. "Mais, I don't see why

you gotta go and jump all over him like that."

"Was I talking to you, Sonny, because I don't think I was. I was talking to Luke, okay? So why don't you stop telling me how to raise my son and go put away the picnic basket. It's in the way."

The white wicker basket still sat at the back of the boat where it'd been when the trawl net snagged. They'd just finished lunch before it happened, before Mr. Sonnier had had a chance to stow the basket below deck. Mr. Sonnier looked toward the basket now, but he didn't move. While Mr. Sonnier was physically bigger than Luke's father, Luke's father was big in a more frightening way. Luke once saw men larger than his father step aside as he and his father walked down the sidewalk in town. Mr. Sonnier might have been tall with an enormous belly, but there wasn't anything threatening about him. He was always reading books, even on the boat.

"You still standing there?" Luke's father said to Mr. Sonnier in a way that Luke could tell was meant to sound hurtful.

"Yeah, I'm still standin' here," Mr. Sonnier said.

Luke liked that Mr. Sonnier always stood up for him, but he hated it more the way it set off his father.

"Well, what are you waiting for, Luke?" his father said. "Goddamn, boy, let's go. Get your shoes off, unless you're planning on swimming in them."

"C'mon, Tommy. What's a matter with you, uh?" Mr. Sonnier said.

Luke felt Mr. Sonnier's large, heavy arm fall around his neck, feeling like a sack of dog food on his shoulder.

"He's being a baby, that's what's the matter," Luke's father said. "He says he's afraid to go in the water."

"Heck, Tommy," Mr. Sonnier said. "He's what, eleven years old? Cut 'em some slack, uh."

"He's twelve, and you're as bad as his mother," Luke's father said.

Without saying anything, Mr. Sonnier sat on one of the ice chests and started removing his shoes.

"Damnit Sonny, I'm sure," Luke's father said. "Look at you."

"Whatcha mean 'look at me', you son of a buck?" Mr. Sonnier said, cussing the way he cussed, which wasn't really cussing at all.

"Sonny, all I'm saying is you're in no condition."

"And all I'm sayin' is if T-Luke doesn't wanna go in then I don't think he should."

"Luke, I can't believe you're gonna make this old man go in the water."

"Old man?" Mr. Sonnier said. "Mais, I ain't that much older than you.

"Okay, I'll do it," Luke said.

"Mais, you don't have to, no," Mr. Sonnier said.

"I don't mind," Luke said.

Mr. Sonnier stood up and put his arm around Luke's shoulder again. "It's probably no more than ten feet deep. Twelve, tops," he said. "A strong swimmer like you? Mais, you won't have no problem with a shallow dive like that."

Luke looked over the side of the boat, seeing only water as deep as he could see. It looked bottomless. Then he noticed his own reflection, a desperate face rising and falling with the boat that lifted and dropped as the swell continued rolling under them.

"It'll be like diving in the deep end of the pool at the country club," Luke's father said. "You always swim there, don't you?"

"I guess so," Luke admitted.

Luke hadn't thought of it that way. He could stay down at the deep end of that pool a long time. He'd always pretended he was diving in the ocean at the pool and now here he was about to do just that and it was nothing like he'd imagined.

"Yeah, T-Luke, you a fish, boy," Mr. Sonnier said. "Mais, you belong in the ocean."

Luke began to feel good about himself. It was true, he was a good swimmer. Without saying anything, he pulled off his T-shirt. He kicked off his wet tennis shoes, not bothering with the laces. He approached the back corner of the stern from where he would dive.

"Okay, Luke, just follow the rope down," Luke's father instructed. "When you get to the bottom just feel around and see what the net's snagged on. We've stirred up the bottom, so you might not be able to see a whole lot, but you should be able to get an idea just by using your hands."

Luke didn't say anything. He was listening, but not hearing anything his father said.

"Don't try and do everything at once," Mr. Sonnier added. "Come up for air if you need to breathe. And remember to keep clear of the props."

The two men helped Luke up onto the gunwale where he stood looking down at the water. The sun blazed directly overhead and the heat moved up and down his bare back like a lot of hot fingers.

"Take a deep breath, Luke, and hold it," his father said, keeping the flat of his hand against Luke's behind to keep him steady against the toss of the boat.

Luke took three deep breaths. He held the third breath and dove in. Now under water, he didn't open his eyes as he searched blindly with his hand for one of the two descending trawl lines. The water at the surface felt warm. As he found one of the taut ropes and began pulling himself down, the water became steadily cooler, then cold.

He began to feel the same pressure in his ears he always felt at the drain of the country club pool and he figured he was at about ten feet. The sound of the boat's engines had weakened and no longer sounded like a boat's engines anymore. It no longer sounded like it came from above, but rather from a distance, a far away hum.

Luke slowed his progress and, without letting go of the rope, he felt for the bottom with an outstretched hand. But it wasn't there. As he continued down farther, he suddenly felt alone. There didn't seem to be a bottom and he wanted to tell his father. As he began to bring his hand back to the rope, it brushed against something. It startled him and he screamed, releasing a mass of air bubbles that raced toward the surface. He was afraid to open his eyes for fear of what he might see. Using the rope, he darted quickly back toward the surface. The water warmed and the sound of the boat's engines grew stronger and sounded like a boat's engines again. He exploded onto the surface of the water and swam wildly toward the boat. He reached his hand toward Mr. Sonnier who hung an arm over the side. Mr. Sonnier gripped Luke's wrists tightly.

"Hurry!" Luke screamed.

"Dang it, T-Luke, hold still, boy, or I'll lose my grip," Mr. Sonnier said. Then in one motion, Luke was out of the water and standing on deck, gasping for air.

"Mais, Tommy, he's hyperventilatin'," Mr. Sonnier said, not seeming to know what to do, but wanting to do something.

"What's a matter, Luke?" his father said.

"Calm down, T-Luke. Everything's okay, boy," Mr. Sonnier said, rubbing a warming friction back into Luke's chilled arms and shoulders.

Luke, still regaining his breath, looked back over the side of the boat. He was certain he would see something there.

"Luke, what is it?" his father said.

"I don't know," Luke said. "I think something was after

me."

"What do you mean something was after you?" his father said, the concerned look disappearing from his face.

"Mr. Sonnier, didn't you see it?" Luke said. "It was down there and it came after me."

"Mais, I didn't see nuttin', Luke," Mr. Sonnier said. "Was it a big fish? Maybe one of them barracudas? Did you see what it was?"

"I don't know," Luke said. "But it's a lot deeper than ten feet, I can tell you that."

"Heck, Tommy, whatcha think it coulda been, uh?" Mr. Sonnier said, now drying off Luke with a towel that was coarse and mildewed from the long time it'd been in the dankness of the front cabin.

"I think it's his imagination, that's what I think," Luke's father said. "I don't doubt he's scared, that's obvious. But he was scared before he went in."

"Dad, I swear," Luke said.

"This is something you need to get over, son. And the only way to do that is to get back in the water."

"Tommy, you can't," Mr. Sonnier said. "Mais, he's scared to death, him."

"I can't, huh? Watch me."

Mr. Sonnier sat back down on the ice chest and removed his shoes. "You may be able to make him go back in," he said, "but you can't keep me from goin' with him." Mr. Sonnier rose from the ice chest. He struggled to pull off the damp shirt that clung to his wet skin, exposing the tremendous belly that made up so much of his bulk. His stomach hung in folds and was pasty and spotted with random patches of black hair. Without taking off his khaki chinos, Mr. Sonnier approached the stern.

"Sonny, you're not going anywhere, so put your damn

shirt back on," Luke's father said. "This has gone far enough. You're really starting to piss me off."

"It's no big deal, Tommy," Mr. Sonnier said. "Besides, I'm hot. A dip in the ocean'll feel good." He began stretching his large arms, flapping them to the sides. He looked like he would sink straight to the bottom.

"It's okay, Mr. Sonnier," Luke said. "I don't mind trying again."

"See, Sonny, he wants to do it," Lukes father said.

"Then we'll do it together," Mr. Sonnier said. "Mais, it sounds like a two man job, anyway, uh." Mr. Sonnier winked at Luke, before letting himself topple awkwardly over the side of the boat, creating a terrific splash. He disappeared beneath the surface before resurfacing behind the boat. "Ready, Luke?" he said, his pasty skin taking on a greenish hue in the cloudy water.

Luke jumped in next to Mr. Sonnier.

"Be careful, Sonny," Luke's father said. "Don't strain yourself, you old coon-ass."

"Don't you worry 'bout me," Mr. Sonnier said. Then he turned to Luke, "grab you ahold a the rope and follow me."

"Keep an eye on him, Luke," Luke heard his father say. "Be careful."

Mr. Sonnier started counting. On the third breath they both went under. Luke felt around with his eyes closed and found the rope. Mr. Sonnier was directly beneath him and, once more, the water got colder as Luke followed the rope down. His ears began to hurt again. He could feel the movement on the rope that Mr. Sonnier made and could tell the big man still continued down. Luke wasn't afraid the way he'd been when alone and he slowly opened his eyes. He realized he could see for about six or seven feet in all directions. Below him, and in the darkening, yellow murkiness, he saw the large white blur of a figure that was Mr. Sonnier leave the rope.

Before, the rope had been Luke's security, but now his security was Mr. Sonnier and Luke left the rope in pursuit of him. Mr. Sonnier had gotten a little ahead and Luke was losing sight of him. As Luke pushed himself on, he brushed something with his hand. It was unfamiliar to the touch, but only because he'd never felt a trawl net under water before. It didn't take long for him to make that distinction and without panicking he followed the net with his hand and found that it was now arching over him. Then Mr. Sonnier's face appeared a few inches in front of Luke, shouting something in a cloud of air bubbles. It was unclear what he said, but Luke knew they needed to go back. Luke turned and swam as quickly as he could. Once clear of the net, he shot upward. He felt his lungs beginning to burn as he broke the surface. The boat was behind him now, rising and dropping under a swell. Luke turned and swam toward the stern where his father stood searching the water with a hand shielding his eyes. "Where's Mr. Sonnier?" he shouted.

"He was right behind me." Luke struggled to breathe as he got the words out. "We were under the net."

"Oh, God," Luke's father said and without kicking off his shoes he dove in and was underwater.

Luke didn't know what to do. He remained where he was, treading water. Then, two heads appeared on the surface. Luke's father held onto Mr. Sonnier. They both gasped for air, coughing and spitting out water.

"Luke," his father said. "Get back on board and throw us the life ring."

Luke moved as fast as he could to the back of the boat where he found the small step that jutted out there. He rose from the water and hauled himself over the gunwale. He could see that Mr. Sonnier was conscious, but weak. The big man's eyes were tightly shut. Luke tossed the life ring to his father who then gave it to Mr. Sonnier to help him stay afloat. Then Luke unlatched the ladder from a rack on the side panel and quickly hung it over the stern. His father remained in the water, waiting for Mr. Sonnier to regain his strength.

After a while, Mr. Sonnier seemed to catch his breath. "There was at least one other net down there that I guess someone else lost," he said. He began breathing heavily again. He shook his head. "Mais, I didn't realize it 'til we were already under it."

"Don't talk, Sonny," Luke's father said. "I think you had a heart attack."

"I just thank God, me, that T-Luke got out okay," Mr. Sonnier said. Now he looked at Luke, looking like he might cry. It made Luke feel like he might cry. "Mais, I can't bear to think of it," he added. "I don't know what I woulda done."

"Take it easy, Sonny," Luke's father said. "We've got to get you back on the boat."

With the help of Luke's father, Mr. Sonnier slowly ascended the ladder. He paused momentarily at the top rung before rolling heavily over the stern and onto the deck where he lay on his back, his large, wet belly rising and falling as he breathed in deep guttural moans, his eyes tightly shut again.

Luke's father climbed aboard as fast as he could. After pulling up the ladder, he tossed it to the deck. As he moved quickly toward the starboard corner, he tripped over the picnic basket that was still sitting there. "Goddammit," he yelled at the basket, looking like he might kick it. Instead, he picked it up and threw it overboard as far as he could. The basket didn't sink, and as it rolled onto its side its lid fell open, releasing the contents. Luke's father un-cleated the two trawl lines and let them sink to the bottom with the net. Then he hurried to the bow to raise the anchor. He didn't speak the whole time.

Luke still stood there, not knowing what to do. He wanted to go in after the picnic basket. He wanted to bring it back on board.

"Don't just stand there, Luke," his father said. "Prop his head up with something." The urgency in his father's voice scared Luke into action. "C'mon, son, hurry."

Luke propped up Mr. Sonnier's head with the life ring. Luke wanted to say something to him. He wanted to say he was sorry.

With the anchor now on board, Luke's father crouched over Mr. Sonnier. "How you making out, Sonny?"

Mr. Sonnier shook his head. "I've felt better," he said, forcing a weak laugh that came out as a cough. He opened his eyes for the first time since coming back on board. "How fast you think we can make it in?"

"We'll head for Intracoastal City," Luke's father said. "I'll radio ahead for an ambulance."

"You know, T-Luke was right," Mr. Sonnier said. "The bottom is a helluva lot deeper than we figured. It must be the base of an abandoned oil rig or something. Mais, you shouldn't a jumped all over him like that."

"I didn't know," Luke's father said.

"Well, now you know," Mr. Sonnier said. Then he closed his eyes again as tightly as before.

Luke's father didn't look at Luke. He didn't say anything. Then he began moving quickly again, moving toward the helm. He gave the boat full throttle and Luke had to brace himself to keep from falling on top of Mr. Sonnier.

"Luke, take the wheel," Luke heard his father shout, and Luke struggled to approach the controls, fighting against the angle of the boat that was still planing off. His father pointed at a position on the distant shoreline. "Head for that cut, okay? See it? That's Four-Mile Canal. It'll take us to Intra-coastal City."

For the first time Luke realized how serious it was. Now he thought he would cry. "Dad, is he gonna be alright?"

"I don't know," his father said, still not looking at Luke. Luke could tell by the way his father said it that he really didn't know.

"Shouldn't we leave a marker to show where the net is?" Luke said.

"What?" his father said. "What the hell's the matter with you?"

But Luke didn't mean that they should leave a marker so they could come back to reclaim the net. And as the boat headed inland, now free from the trawl lines, Luke looked back at the spot where they'd left the net. The only indication being the white wicker picnic basket in the swirl of water the boat had made in its quick departure. The basket's con-tents—the Styrofoam cartons of potato salad, coleslaw, and pork and beans, the Tupperware containers of ham, cheese, and homemade brownies, and the packages of fancy paper plates and matching yellow napkins—were now all scattered over the water. Moments later the water would smooth over and the picnic basket and all its contents would be carried away by the current. Then the deep oil pit, along with the abandoned trawl nets, would be hidden again, offering no warning of what lay waiting there.

Acknowledgements

Thanks, mom, for always encouraging me to dream and, dad, for urging me to write, even when I didn't want to anymore. Thank you Mike Bales, Chad Berry, Jason Stanfield, Dave McKay, Kent Johnson, Sean McLaughlin, David Coats , Bill Anderson, and Chris Sekin for never hesitating to read my stuff, even long before it was ready. Thank you Brenda and Juliette for your love, support and patience, and for putting up with me when you have every right not to. Thank you James D. Wilson and UL Press for taking a chance on an unknown. Dan Hale, *je vous remercie d'être là pour moi tout au long du voyage*. And finally, thank you John Ed Bradley, my friend, my mentor and my brother, for without whom I would never have first put pen to paper. We did it, Papa. The events and characters depicted in these stories are fictional, but southwest Louisiana, and my hometown of Abbeville, in particular, is the real deal.

Gratefully acknowledged are the journals in which these stories originally appeared: "Duck Thief" appeared in *South Dakota Review*; "A Changed Man" appeared in *Saint Ann's Review*; "A Return To Glencoe" appeared in *Los Angeles Review*; "Nostrils" appeared in *Prick of the Spindle*; "Big Damn Pears" appeared in *The Dos Passos Review* and then again in *Deep South Magazine*; "The Way You Really Are?" appeared in *Pear Noir* and again in *Rosebud Magazine*; "Christmas Eve" appeared in *Lost in Thought*; "Bayou Noir" appeared in *Big Muddy*; "Voyeurs" appeared in *Conclave: a Journal of Character*; "Rendezvous" appeared in *The MacGuffin*; and "Trawling" appeared in *Green Hills Literary Lantern*.

About the Author

David Langlinais has published stories in numerous journals, including *South Dakota Review*, *Los Angeles Review*, *The Dos Passos Review*, *Big Muddy*, *Deep South Magazine* and *The MacGuffin*. Born and raised in Abbeville, Louisiana, he currently lives in Dallas with his wife, Brenda, and daughter, Juliette, where he works as a freelance copywriter.

UNIVERSITY OF LOUISIANA AT LAFAYETTE PRESS

LOUISIANA WRITERS SERIES

The Louisiana Writers Series is dedicated to publishing works that present Louisiana's diverse creative and cultural heritage. The series includes poetry, short stories, essays, creative nonfiction, and novels.

BOOKS IN THE LOUISIANA WRITERS SERIES:

The Blue Boat by Darrell Bourque (out of print)
Amid the Swirling Ghosts by William Caverlee
Local Hope by Jack Heflin
New Orleans: What Can't Be Lost edited by Lee Barclay
In Ordinary Light by Darrell Bourque
Higher Ground by James Nolan
Dirty Rice: A Season in the Evangeline League by Gerald Duff
Megan's Guitar and Other Poems from Acadie by Darrell Bourque
The Land Baron's Sun by Genaro Smith
You Don't Know Me: New and Selected Stories by James Nolan
Duck Thief and Other Stories by David Langlinais
Dead Dog Lying and Other Stories by Norman German

FOR MORE INFORMATION VISIT:
WWW.ULPRESS.ORG